"You can ask me anything, princess," Rodolfo heard himself say.

In a lazy, smoky sort of tone he'd never used in her presence before. Because this was the princess he was going to marry, not one of the enterprising women who flung themselves at him everywhere he went, looking for a taste of Europe's favorite daredevil prince.

There was no denying it. Suddenly, out of nowhere, he wanted his future wife.

Desperately.

As if she could tell—as if she'd somehow become the sort of woman who could read a man's desire and use it against him, when he'd have sworn she was anything but—Valentina's smile deepened.

She tilted her head to one side. "It's about your shocking double standard," she said sweetly. "If you can cat your way through all of Europe, why can't I?"

Something black and wild and wholly unfamiliar surged in him then, making Rodolfo's hands curl into fists and his entire body go tense, taut.

Then he really shocked the hell out of himself.

"Because," he all but snarled, and there was no pretending that wasn't exactly what he was doing. No matter how unlikely. "Like it or not, princess, you are mine."

Caitlin Crews

THE PRINCE'S NINE-MONTH SCANDAL

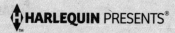

Recycling programs
for this product may
not exist in your area.

ISBN-13: 978-0-373-06074-0

The Prince's Nine-Month Scandal

First North American Publication 2017

Copyright © 2017 by Caitlin Crews

Printed in U.S.A.

USA TODAY bestselling and RITA® Award–nominated author **Caitlin Crews** loves writing romance. She teaches her favorite romance novels in creative writing classes at places like UCLA Extension's prestigious Writers' Program, where she finally gets to utilize the MA and PhD in English literature she received from the University of York in England. She currently lives in California, with her very own hero and too many pets. Visit her at caitlincrews.com.

Visit the Author Profile page at Harlequin.com for more titles.

CHAPTER ONE

NATALIE MONETTE HAD never done a rash thing in her entire twenty-seven years, something she'd always viewed as a great personal strength. After a childhood spent flitting about with her free-spirited, impetuous mother, never belonging anywhere and without a shred of anything resembling permanence including an address, Natalie had made her entire adulthood—especially her career—a monument to all things *dependable* and *predictable*.

But she'd finally had enough.

Her employer—never an easy man at the best of times—wasn't likely to accept her notice after five long years with anything like grace. Natalie shook her head at the very notion of grace and her cranky billionaire boss. He preferred a bull-in-china-shop approach to most things, especially his executive assistant. And this latest time, as he'd dressed her down for an imagined mistake in front of an entire corporate office in London, a little voice inside her had whispered: *enough.*

Enough already. Or she thought she might die. Internally, anyway.

She had to quit her job. She had to figure out what her life was like when not at the beck and call of a tyrant—because there had to be better things out there. There had to be. She had to do *something* before she just…disappeared.

And she was thinking that a rash move—like quitting here and now and who cared if her boss threw a tantrum?—might just do the trick.

Natalie was washing her hands in the marbled sink in the fancy women's bathroom that was a part of the moneyed elegance evident everywhere in the high-class lounge area at her boss's preferred private airfield outside London. She was trying to slow her panicked breathing and get herself back under control. She prided herself on being unflappable under normal circumstances, but nothing about the messy things swirling around inside of her today felt *normal*. She hardly paid any attention when one of the heavy stall doors behind her opened and a woman stepped up to the sink beside hers. She had the vague impression of the sort of marked glamour that was usually on display in these places she only visited thanks to her job, but then went back to wondering how on earth she was going to walk out of this bathroom and announce that she was done with her job.

She couldn't imagine how her boss would react. Or she could, that was the trouble. But Natalie knew she had to do it. *She had to do it.* Now, while there was still this feverish thing inside her that kept pushing at her. Because if she waited, she knew she wouldn't. She'd settle back in and it would be another five years in an instant, and then what would she do?

"I beg your pardon, but you seem to look a great deal like someone I know."

The woman's voice was cultured. Elegant. And it made Natalie feel...funny. As if she'd heard it before when she knew that was impossible. Of course she hadn't. She never knew anyone in these ultra high-class places her job took her. Then she looked up and the world seemed to tilt off its axis. She was shocked she didn't crumple to the ground where she stood.

Because the woman standing beside her, staring back at her through the mirror, had her face. *The exact same face.* Her coppery hair was styled differently and she wasn't wearing Natalie's dark-rimmed glasses over her own green eyes, but there was no denying that every other aspect was *exactly the same.* The fine nose. The faintly pointed chin. The same raised eyebrows, the same high forehead.

The other woman was taller, Natalie realized in a rush of something more complicated than simple relief. But then she looked down to see that her impossible, improbable twin was wearing the sort of sky-high stilettos only women who didn't have to walk very often or very far enjoyed, easily making her a few inches taller than Natalie in the far more serviceable wedges she wore that allowed her to keep up with her irascible employer's long, impatient stride.

"Oh." The other woman breathed the syllable out, like a sigh, though her eyes gleamed. "I thought there was an amusing resemblance that we should discuss, but this…"

Natalie had the bizarre experience of watching her own mouth move on another woman's face. Then drop open slightly. It was unnerving. It was like the mirror coming alive right in front of her. It was *impossible*.

It was a great deal more than an "amusing resemblance."

"What is this?" she asked, her voice as shaky as she felt. "How…?"

"I have no idea," the other woman said quietly. "But it's fascinating, isn't it?" She turned to look at Natalie directly, letting her gaze move up and down her body as if measuring her. Cataloging her. Natalie could hardly blame her. If she wasn't so frozen, she'd do the same. "I'm Valentina."

"Natalie."

Why was her throat so dry? But she knew why. They said everyone on earth had a double, but that was usually a discussion about mannerisms and a vague resemblance. Not *this*. Because Natalie knew beyond the shadow of any possible doubt that there was no way this person standing in front of her, with the same eyes and the same mouth and even the same freckle centered on her left cheekbone wasn't related to her. No possible way. And that was a Pandora's box full of problems, wasn't it? Starting with her own childhood and the mother who had always rather sternly claimed she didn't know who Natalie's father was. She tried to shake all that off—but then Valentina's name penetrated her brain.

She remembered where she was. And the other party that had been expected at the same airfield today. She'd openly scoffed at the notification, because there wasn't much on this earth she found more useless than royalty. Her mother had gotten that ball rolling while Natalie was young. While other girls had dressed up like princesses and dreamed about Prince Charming, Natalie had been taught that both were lies.

There's no such thing as happily-ever-after, her mother had told her. *There's only telling a silly story about painful things to make yourself feel better. No daughter of mine is going to imagine herself anything but a realist, Natalie.*

And so Natalie hadn't. Ever.

Here in this bathroom, face-to-face with an impossibility, Natalie blinked. "Wait. You're that princess."

"I am indeed, for my sins." Valentina's mouth curved in a serene sort of half smile that Natalie would have said she, personally, could never pull off. Except if someone with an absolutely identical face could do it, that meant she could, too, didn't it?

That realization was…unnerving. "But I suspect you might be, too."

Natalie couldn't process that. Her eyes were telling her a truth, but her mind couldn't accept it. She played devil's advocate instead. "We can't possibly be related. I'm a glorified secretary who never really had a home. You're a royal princess. Presumably your lineage—and the family home, for that matter, which I'm pretty sure is a giant castle because all princesses have a few of those by virtue of the title alone—dates back to the Roman Conquest."

"Give or take a few centuries." Valentina inclined her head, another supremely elegant and vaguely noble gesture that Natalie would have said could only look silly on her. Yet it didn't look anything like silly on Valentina. "Depending which branch of the family you mean, of course."

"I was under the impression that people with lineages that could lead to thrones and crown jewels tended to keep better track of their members."

"You'd think, wouldn't you?" The princess shifted back on her soaring heels and regarded Natalie more closely. "Conspiracy theorists claim my mother was killed and the death hushed up. Senior palace officials assured me that no, she merely left to preserve her mental health, and is rumored to be in residence in a hospital devoted to such things somewhere. All I know is that I haven't seen her since shortly after I was born. According to my father, she preferred anonymity to the joys of motherhood."

Natalie wanted to run out of this bathroom, lose herself in her work and her boss's demands the way she usually did, and pretend this mad situation had never happened. This encounter felt rash enough for her as it was. No need to blow her life up on top of it. So she had no idea why instead, she opened up her mouth and shared her deepest, secret shame with this woman.

"I've never met my father," she told this total stranger who looked like an upscale mirror image of herself. There was no reason she should feel as if she could trust a random woman she met in a bathroom, no matter whose face she wore. It was absurd to feel as if she'd known this other person all her life when of course she hadn't. And yet she kept talking. "My mother's always told me she has no idea who he was. That Prince Charming was a fantasy sold to impressionable young girls to make them silly, and the reality was that men are simply men and untrustworthy to the core. And she bounces from one affair to the next pretty quickly, so I came to terms with the fact it was possible she really, truly didn't know."

Valentina laughed. It was a low, smoky sound, and Natalie recognized it, because it was hers. A shock of recognition went through her. Though she didn't feel like laughing. At all.

"My father is many things," the princess said, laughter and something more serious beneath it. "Including His Royal Majesty, King Geoffrey of Murin.

What he is not now, nor has ever been, I imagine, is forgettable."

Natalie shook her head. "You underestimate my mother's commitment to amnesia. She's made it a life choice instead of a malady. On some level I admire it."

Once again, she had no idea why she was telling this stranger things she hardly dared admit to herself.

"My mother was the noblewoman Frederica de Burgh, from a very old Murinese family." Valentina watched Natalie closely as she spoke. "Promised to my father at birth, raised by nuns and kept deliberately sheltered, and then widely held to be unequal to the task of becoming queen. Mentally. But that's the story they would tell, isn't it, to explain why she disappeared? What's your mother's name?"

Her hands felt numb, so Natalie shifted her bag from her shoulder to the marble countertop beside her. "She calls herself Erica."

For a moment neither one of them spoke. Neither one of them mentioned that *Erica* sounded very much like a shortened form of *Frederica,* but then, there was no need. Natalie was aware of too many things. The far-off sounds of planes outside the building. The television in the lounge on the other side of the door, cued to a twenty-four-hour news channel. She was vaguely surprised her boss hadn't already texted her fifteen furious times, wondering where she'd gone off to when it was possible he might have need of her.

"I saw everyone's favorite billionaire, Achilles Casilieris, out there in the lounge," Valentina said after a moment, as if reading Natalie's mind. "He looks even more fearsome in person than advertised. You can almost *see* all that brash command and dizzying wealth ooze from his pores, can't you?"

"He's my boss." Natalie ran her tongue over her teeth, that reckless thing inside of her lurching to life all over again. "If he was really oozing anything, anywhere, it would be my job to provide first aid until actual medical personnel could come handle it. At which point he would bite my head off for wasting his precious time by not curing him instantly."

She had worked for Achilles Casilieris—and by extension the shockingly hardy, internationally envied and recession-proof Casilieris Company—for five very long years. That was the first marginally negative thing she'd said about her job, ever. Out loud, anyway. And she felt instantly disloyal, despite the fact she'd been psyching herself up to quit only moments ago. Much as she had when she'd opened her mouth about her mother.

How could a stranger who happened to look like her make Natalie question who *she* was?

But the princess was frowning at the slim leather clutch she'd tossed on the bathroom counter. Natalie heard the buzzing sound that indicated a call as Valentina flipped open the outer flap and slid her smartphone out, then rolled her eyes and shoved it back in.

"My fiancé," she said, meeting Natalie's gaze

again, her own more guarded. Or maybe it was something else that made the green in her eyes darker. The phone buzzed a few more times, then stopped. "Or his chief of staff, to be more precise."

"Congratulations," Natalie said, though the expression on Valentina's face did not look as if she was precisely awash in joyous anticipation.

"Thank you, I'm very lucky." Valentina's mouth curved, though there was nothing like a smile in her eyes and her tone was arid. "Everyone says so. Prince Rodolfo is objectively attractive. Not all princes can make that claim, but the tabloids have exulted over his abs since he was a teenager. Just as they have salivated over his impressive dating history, which has involved a selection of models and actresses from at least four continents and did not cease in any noticeable way upon our engagement last fall."

"Your Prince Charming sounds…charming," Natalie murmured. It only confirmed her long-held suspicions about such men.

Valentina raised one shoulder, then dropped it. "His theory is that he remains free until our marriage, and then will be free once again following the necessary birth of his heir. More discreetly, I can only hope. Meanwhile, I am beside myself with joy that I must take my place at his side in two short months. Of course."

Natalie didn't know why she laughed at that, but she did. More out of commiseration than anything else, as if they really were the same person. And how strange that she almost felt as if they were. "It's going to be a terrific couple of months all around, then. Mr. Casilieris is in rare form. He's putting together a particularly dramatic deal and it's not going his way and he…isn't used to that. So that's me working twenty-two-hour days instead of my usual twenty for the foreseeable future, which is even more fun when he's cranky and snarling."

"It can't possibly be worse than having to smile politely while your future husband lectures you about the absurd expectation of fidelity in what is essentially an arranged marriage for hours on end. The absurdity is that *he* might be expected to curb his impulses for a year or so, in case you wondered. The expectations for *me* apparently involve quietly and chastely finding fulfillment in philanthropic works, like his sainted absentee mother who everyone knows manufactured a supposed health crisis so she could live out her days in peaceful seclusion. It's easy to be philanthropically fulfilled while living in isolation in Bavaria."

Natalie smiled. "Try biting your tongue while your famously short-tempered boss rages at you for no reason, for the hundredth time in an hour, because he pays you to stand there and take it without wilting or crying or selling whinging stories about him to the press."

Valentina's smile was a perfect match. "Or the hours and hours of grim palace-vetted pre-wedding press interviews in the company of a pack of advisors who will censor everything I say and inevitably make me sound like a bit of animated treacle, as out of touch with reality as the average overly sweet dessert."

"Speaking of treats, I also have to deal with the board of directors Mr. Casilieris treats like irritating schoolchildren, his packs of furious ex-lovers each with her own vendetta, all his terrified employees who need to be coached through meetings with him and treated for PTSD after, and every last member of his staff in every one of his households, who like me to be the one to ask him the questions they know will set him off on one of his scorch-the-earth rages."

They'd moved a little bit closer then, leaning toward each other like friends. *Or sisters,* a little voice whispered. It should have concerned Natalie like everything else about this. And like everything else, it did and it didn't. Either way, she didn't step back. She didn't insist upon her personal space. She was almost tempted to imagine her body knew something about this mirror image version of her that her brain was still desperately trying to question.

Natalie thought of the way Mr. Casilieris had bitten her head off earlier, and her realization that if she didn't escape him now she never would. And how this stranger with her face seemed, oddly enough, to understand.

"I was thinking of quitting, to be honest," she whispered. Making it real. "Today."

"I can't quit, I'm afraid," the impossibly glamorous princess said then, her green eyes alight with something a little more frank than plain mischief. "But I have a better idea. Let's switch places. For a month, say. Six weeks at the most. Just for a little break."

"That's crazy," Natalie said.

"Insane," Valentina agreed. "But you might find royal protocol exciting! And I've always wanted to do the things everyone else in the world does. Like go to a real job."

"People can't *switch places*." Natalie was frowning. "And certainly not with a princess."

"You could think about whether or not you really want to quit," Valentina pointed out. "It would be a lovely holiday for you. Where will Achilles Casilieris be in six weeks' time?"

"He's never gone from London for too long," Natalie heard herself say, as if she was considering it.

Valentina smiled. "Then in six weeks we'll meet in London. We'll text in the meantime with all the necessary details about our lives, and on the appointed day we'll just meet up and switch back and no one will ever be the wiser. Doesn't that sound like *fun*?" Her gaze met Natalie's with something like compassion. "And I hope you won't mind my saying this, but you do look as if you could use a little fun."

"It would never work." Natalie realized after she spoke that she still hadn't said no. "No one will ever believe I'm you."

Valentina waved a hand between them. "How

would anyone know the difference? I can barely tell myself."

"People will take one look at me and know I'm not you," Natalie insisted, as if that was the key issue here. "You look like a *princess*."

If Valentina noticed the derisive spin she put on that last word out of habit, she appeared to ignore it.

"You too can look like a princess. This princess, anyway. You already do."

"There's a lifetime to back it up. You're elegant. Poised. You've had years of training, presumably. How to be a diplomat. How to be polite in every possible situation. Which fork to use at dinner, for God's sake."

"Achilles Casilieris is one of the wealthiest men alive. He dines with as many kings as I do. I suspect that as his personal assistant, Natalie, you have, too. And have likely learned how to navigate the cutlery."

"No one will believe it," Natalie whispered, but there was no heat in it.

Because maybe she was the one who couldn't believe it. And maybe, if she was entirely honest, there was a part of her that wanted this. The princess life and everything that went with it. The kind of ease she'd never known—and a castle besides. And only for a little while. Six short weeks. Scarcely more than a daydream.

Surely even Natalie deserved a daydream. Just this once.

Valentina's smile widened as if she could scent

capitulation in the air. She tugged off the enormous, eye-gouging ring on her left hand and placed it down on the counter between them. It made an audible *clink* against the marble surface.

"Try it on. I dare you. It's an heirloom from Prince Rodolfo's extensive treasury of such items, dating back to the dawn of time, more or less." She inclined her head in that regal way of hers. "If it doesn't fit we'll never speak of switching places again."

And Natalie felt possessed by a force she didn't understand. She knew better. Of course she did. This was a ridiculous game and it could only make this bizarre situation worse, and she was certainly no Cinderella. She knew that much for sure.

But she slipped the ring onto her finger anyway, and it fit perfectly, gleaming on her finger like every dream she'd ever had as a little girl. Not that she could live a magical life, filled with talismans that shone the way this ring did, because that was the sort of *impracticality* her mother had abhorred. But that she could have a home the way everyone else did. That she could *belong* to a man, to a country, to the sweep of a long history, the way this ring hugged her finger. As if it was meant to be.

The ring had nothing to do with her. She knew that. But it felt like a promise, even so.

And it all seemed to snowball from there. They each kicked off their shoes and stood barefoot on the surprisingly plush carpet. Then Valentina shimmied out of her sleek, deceptively simple sheath dress with the unselfconsciousness of a woman used to being dressed by attendants. She lifted her brows with all the imperiousness of her station, and Natalie found herself retreating into the stall with the dress—since she was not, in fact, used to being tended to by packs of fawning courtiers and therefore all but naked with an audience. She climbed out of her own clothes, handing her pencil skirt, blouse and wrap sweater out to Valentina through the crack she left open in the door. Then she tugged the princess's dress on, expecting it to snag or pull against her obviously peasant body.

But like the ring, the dress fit as if it had been tailored to her body. As if it was hers.

She walked out slowly, blinking when she saw... herself waiting for her. The very same view she'd seen in the mirror this morning when she'd dressed in the room Mr. Casilieris kept for her in the basement of his London town house because her own small flat was too far away to be to-ing and fro-ing at odd hours, according to him, and it was easier to acquiesce than fight. Not that it had kept him from firing away at her. But she shoved that aside because Valentina was laughing at the sight of Natalie in obvious astonishment, as if she was having the same literal out-of-body experience.

Natalie walked back to the counter and climbed into the princess's absurd shoes, very carefully. Her knees protested beneath her as she tried to stand tall in them and she had to reach out to grip the marble counter.

"Put your weight on your heels," Valentina advised. She was already wearing Natalie's wedges, because apparently even their feet were the same, and of course she had no trouble standing in them as if she'd picked them out herself. "Everyone always wants to lean forward and tiptoe in heels like that, and nothing looks worse. Lean back and you own the shoe, not the other way around." She eyed Natalie. "Will your glasses give me a headache, do you suppose?"

Natalie pulled them from her face and handed them over. "They're clear glass. I was getting a little too much attention from some of the men Mr. Casilieris works with, and it annoyed him. I didn't want to lose my job, so I started wearing my hair up and these glasses. It worked like a charm."

"I refuse to believe men are so idiotic."

Natalie grinned as Valentina took the glasses and slid them onto her nose. "The men we're talking about weren't exactly paying me attention because they found me enthralling. It was a diversionary tactic during negotiations and yes, you'd be surprised how many men fail to see a woman who looks smart."

She tugged her hair tie from her ponytail and shook out her hair, then handed the elastic to Valentina. The princess swept her hair back and into the same ponytail Natalie had been sporting only seconds before.

And it was like magic.

Ordinary Natalie Monette, renowned for her fierce work ethic, attention to detail and her total lack of anything resembling a personal life—which was how she'd become the executive assistant to one of the world's most ferocious and feared billionaires straight out of college and now had absolutely no life to call her own—became Her Royal Highness, Princess Valentina of Murin in an instant. And vice versa. Just like that.

"This is crazy," Natalie whispered.

The real Princess Valentina only smiled, looking every inch the smooth, super competent right hand of a man as feared as he was respected. Looking the way Natalie had always *hoped* she looked, if she was honest. Serenely capable. Did this mean… she always had?

More than that, they looked like twins. They had to be twins. There was no possibility that they could be anything but.

Natalie didn't want to think about the number of lies her mother had to have told her if that was true. She didn't want to think about all the implications. She couldn't.

"We have to switch places now," Valentina said softly, though there was a catch in her voice. It was the catch that made Natalie focus on her rather than the mystery that was her mother. "I've always wanted to be…someone else. Someone normal. Just for a little while."

Their gazes caught at that, both the exact same shade of green, just as their hair was that unusual shade of copper many tried to replicate in the salon, yet couldn't. The only difference was that Valentina's was highlighted with streaks of blond that Natalia suspected came from long, lazy days on the decks of yachts or taking in the sunshine from the comfort of her very own island kingdom.

If you're really twins—if you're sisters—it's your island, too, a little voice inside whispered. But Natalie couldn't handle that. Not here. Not now. Not while she was all dressed up in princess clothes.

"Is that what princesses dream of?" Natalie asked. She wanted to smile, but the moment felt too precarious. Ripe and swollen with emotions she couldn't have named, though she understood them as they moved through her. "Because I think most other little girls imagine they're you."

Not her, of course. Never her.

Something shone a little too brightly in Valentina's gaze then, and it made Natalie's chest ache.

But she would never know what her mirror image might have said next, because her name was called in a familiar growl from directly outside the door to the women's room. Natalie didn't think. She was dressed as someone else and she couldn't let anyone see that—so she threw herself back into the stall where she'd changed her clothes as the door was slapped open.

"Exactly what are you doing in here?" growled a voice that Natalie knew better than her own. She'd worked for Achilles Casilieris for five years. She knew him much, much better than she knew herself. She knew, for example, that the particular tone he was using right now meant his usual grouchy mood was being rapidly taken over by his typical impatience. He'd likely had to actually take a moment and look for her, rather than her magically being at his side before he finished his thought. He hated that. And he wasn't shy at all about expressing his feelings. "Can we leave for New York now, do you think, or do you need to fix your makeup for another hour?"

Natalie stood straighter out of habit, only to realize that her boss's typical scowl wasn't directed at her. She was hidden behind the cracked open door of the bathroom stall. Her boss was aiming that famous glare straight at Valentina, and he didn't appear to notice that she wasn't Natalie. That if she was Natalie, that would mean she'd lightened her hair in the past fifteen minutes. But she could tell that all her boss saw was his assistant. Nothing more, nothing less.

"I apologize," Valentina murmured.

"I don't need you to be sorry, I need you on the plane," Achilles retorted, then turned back around to head out.

Natalie's head spun. She had worked for this man, night and day, for *half a decade*. He was Achilles Casilieris, renowned for his keen insight and killer instincts in all things, and Natalie had absolutely no doubt that he had no idea that he hadn't been speaking to her.

Maybe that was why, when Valentina reached over and took Natalie's handbag instead of her own, Natalie didn't push back out of the stall to stop her. She said nothing. She stood where she was. She did absolutely nothing to keep the switch from happening.

"I'll call you," Valentina mouthed into the mirror as she hurried to the door, and the last Natalie saw of Her Royal Highness Valentina of Murin was the suppressed excitement in her bright green eyes as she followed Achilles Casilieris out the door.

Natalie stepped out of the stall again in the sudden silence. She looked at herself in the mirror, smoothed her hair down with palms that shook only the slightest little bit, blinked at the wild sparkle of the absurd ring on her finger as she did it.

And just like that, became a fairy princess—and stepped right into a daydream.

CHAPTER TWO

CROWN PRINCE RODOLFO of the ancient and deeply, deliberately reserved principality of Tissely, tucked away in the Pyrenees between France and Spain and gifted with wealth, peace and dramatic natural borders that had kept things that way for centuries untold, was bored.

This was not his preferred state of existence, though it was not exactly surprising here on the palace grounds of Murin Castle, where he was expected to entertain the royal bride his father had finally succeeded in forcing upon him.

Not that "entertainment" was ever really on offer with the undeniably pretty, yet almost aggressively placid and unexciting Princess Valentina. His future wife. The future mother of his children. His future queen, even. Assuming he didn't lapse into a coma before their upcoming nuptials, that was.

Rodolfo sighed and stretched out his long legs, aware he was far too big to be sitting so casually on a relic of a settee in this stuffily proper reception room that had been set aside for his use on one of his set monthly visits with his fiancée. He still felt a twinge in one thigh from the ill-advised diving trip he'd taken some months back with a group of his friends and rather too many sharks. Rodolfo rubbed at the scarred spot absently, grateful that while his father had inevitably caught wind of the feminine talent who'd graced the private yacht off the coast of Belize, the fact an overenthusiastic shark had grazed the Crown Prince of Tissely en route to a friend's recently caught fish had escaped both the King's spies' and the rabid tabloids' breathless reports.

It was these little moments of unexpected grace, he often thought with varying degrees of irony, that made his otherwise royally pointless life worth living.

"You embarrass yourself more with each passing year," his father had told him, stiff with fury, when Rodolfo had succumbed to the usual demands for a command appearance upon his return to Europe at the end of last summer, the salacious pictures of his "Belize Booze Cruise" still fresh in every tabloid reader's mind. And more to the point, in his father's.

"You possess the power to render me unembarrassing forevermore," Rodolfo had replied easily enough. He'd almost convinced himself his father no longer got beneath his skin. Almost. "Give me something to do, Father. You have an entire kingdom at your disposal. Surely you can find a single task for your only son."

But that was the crux of the matter they never spoke of directly, of course. Rodolfo was not the son his father had wanted as heir. He was not the son his father would have chosen to succeed him, not the son his father had planned for. He was his father's only *remaining* son, and not his father's choice.

He was not Felipe. He could never be Felipe. It was a toss-up as to which one of them hated him more for that.

"There is no place in my kingdom for a sybaritic fool whose life is little more than an extended advertisement for one of those appalling survival programs, complete with the sensationalism of the nearest gutter press," his father had boomed from across his vast, appropriately majestic office in the palace, because it was so much easier to attack Rodolfo than address what simmered beneath it all. Not that Rodolfo helped matters with his increasingly dangerous antics, he was aware. "You stain the principality with every astonishingly bad decision you make."

"It was a boat ride, sir." Rodolfo had kept his voice even because he knew it irritated his father to get no reaction to his litanies and insults. "Not precisely a scandal likely to topple the whole of the kingdom's government, as I think you are aware."

"What I am aware of, as ever, is how precious little you know about governing anything," his father had seethed, in all his state and consequence.

"You could change that with a wave of your hand," Rodolfo had reminded him, as gently as possible. Which was perhaps not all that gently. "Yet you refuse."

And around and around they went.

Rodolfo's father, the taciturn and disapproving sovereign of Tissely, Ferdinand IV, held all the duties of the monarchy in his tight fists and showed no signs of easing his grip anytime soon. Despite the promise he'd made his only remaining son and heir that he'd give him a more than merely ceremonial place in the principality's government following Rodolfo's graduate work at the London School of Economics. That had been ten years back, his father had only grown more bitter and possessive of his throne, and Rodolfo had…adapted.

Life in the principality was sedate, as befitted a nation that had avoided all the wars of the last few centuries by simple dint of being too far removed to take part in them in any real way. Rodolfo's life, by contrast, was…stimulating. Provocative by design. He liked his sport extreme and his sex excessive, and he didn't much care if the slavering hounds of the European press corps printed every moment of each, which they'd been more than happy to do for the past decade. If his father wished him to be more circumspect, to preserve and protect the life of the hereditary heir to Tissely's throne the way he should—the way he'd raced about trying to wrap Felipe in cotton wool, restricting him from everything only to lose him to something as ignoble and silly as an unremarkable cut in his finger and what they'd thought was the flu—he needed only to offer Rodolfo something else with which to fill his time. Such as, perhaps, something to *do* besides continue to exist, thus preserving the bloodline by dint of not dying.

In fairness, of course, Rodolfo had committed himself to pushing the boundaries of his continued existence as much as possible, with his group of similarly devil-may-care friends, to the dismay of most of their families.

"Congratulations," Ferdinand had clipped out one late September morning last fall in yet another part of his vast offices in the Tisselian palace complex. "You will be married next summer."

"I beg your pardon?"

In truth, Rodolfo had not been paying much attention to the usual lecture until that moment. He was no fan of being summoned from whatever corner of the world he happened to be inhabiting and having to race back to present himself before Ferdinand, because his lord and father preferred not to communicate with his only heir by any other means but face-to-face. But of course, Ferdinand had not solicited his opinion. Ferdinand never did.

When he'd focused on his father, sitting there behind the acres and acres of his desk, the old man had actually looked...smug.

That did not bode well.

"You've asked me for a role in the kingdom and here it is. The Crown Prince of Tissely has been unofficially betrothed to the Murin princess since her birth. It is high time you did your duty and ensured the line. This should not come as any great surprise. You are not exactly getting any younger, Rodolfo, as your increasingly more desperate public displays amply illustrate."

Rodolfo had let that deliberate slap roll off his back, because there was no point reacting. It was what his father wanted.

"I met the Murin princess exactly once when I was ten and she was in diapers." Felipe had been fourteen and a man of the world, to Rodolfo's recollection, and the then Crown Prince of Tissely had seemed about as unenthused about his destiny as Rodolfo felt now. "That seems a rather tenuous connection upon which to base a marriage, given I've never seen her since."

"Princess Valentina is renowned the world over for her commitment to her many responsibilities and her role as her father's emissary," his father had replied coolly. "I doubt your paths would have crossed in all these years, as she is not known to frequent the dens of iniquity you prefer."

"Yet you believe this paragon will wish to marry me."

"I am certain she will wish no such thing, but the princess is a dutiful creature who knows what she owes to her country. You claim that you are as well, and that your dearest wish is to serve the crown. Now is your chance to prove it."

And that was how Rodolfo had found himself both hoist by his own petard and more worrying, tied to his very proper, very dutiful, very, very boring bride-to-be with no hope of escape. Ever.

"Princess Valentina, Your Highness," the butler

intoned from the doorway, and Rodolfo dutifully climbed to his feet, because his life might have been slipping out of his control by the second, but hell, he still had the manners that had been beaten into him since he was small.

The truth was, he'd imagined that he would do things differently than his father when he'd realized he would have to take Felipe's place as the heir to his kingdom. He'd been certain he would not marry a woman he hardly knew, foisted upon him by duty and immaculate bloodlines, with whom he could hardly carry on a single meaningful conversation. His own mother—no more enamored of King Ferdinand than Rodolfo was—had long since repaired to her preferred residence, her ancestral home in the manicured wilds of Bavaria, and had steadfastly maintained an enduring if vague health crisis that necessitated she remain in seclusion for the past twenty years.

Rodolfo had been so sure, as an angry young man still reeling from his brother's death, that he would do things better when he had his chance.

And instead he was standing attendance on a strange woman who, in the months of their engagement, had appeared to be made entirely of impenetrable glass. She was about that approachable.

But this time, when Valentina walked into the reception room the way she'd done many times before, so they could engage in a perfectly tedious hour of perfectly polite conversation on perfectly pointless topics as if it was the stifling sixteenth century, all to allow the waiting press corps to gush about their visits later as they caught Rodolfo leaving, everything…changed.

Rodolfo couldn't have said how. Much less why.

But he *felt* her entrance. He *felt it* when she paused in the doorway and looked around as if she'd never laid eyes on him or the paneled ceiling or any part of the run-of-the-mill room before. His body tightened. He felt a rush of heat pool in his—

Impossible.

What the hell was happening to him?

Rodolfo felt his gaze narrow as he studied his fiancée. She looked the way she always did, and yet she didn't. She wore one of her efficiently sophisticated and chicly demure ensembles, a deceptively simple sheath dress that showed nothing and yet obliquely drew attention to the sheer feminine perfection of her form. A form he'd seen many times before, always clothed beautifully, and yet had never found himself waxing rhapsodic about before. Yet today he couldn't look away. There was something about the way she stood, as if she was unsteady on those cheeky heels she wore, though that seemed unlikely. Her hair flowed around her shoulders and looked somehow wilder than it usually did, as if the copper of it was redder. Or perhaps brighter.

Or maybe he needed to get his head examined. Maybe he really had gotten a concussion when he'd gone on an impromptu skydiving trip last week, tumbling a little too much on his way down into the remotest peaks of the Swiss Alps.

The princess moistened her lips and then met his gaze, and Rodolfo felt it like her sultry little mouth all over the hardest part of him.

What the hell?

"Hello," she said, and even her voice was…different, somehow. He couldn't put his finger on it. "It's lovely to see you."

"Lovely to see me?" he echoed, astonished. And something far more earthy, if he was entirely honest with himself. "Are you certain? I was under the impression you would prefer a rousing spot of dental surgery to another one of these meetings. I feel certain you almost admitted as much at our last one."

He didn't know what had come over him. He'd managed to maintain his civility throughout all these months despite his creeping boredom—what had changed today? He braced himself, expecting the perfect princess to collapse into an offended heap on the polished floor, which he'd have a hell of a time explaining to her father, the humorless King Geoffrey of Murin.

But Valentina only smiled and a gleam he'd never seen before kindled in her eyes, which he supposed must always have been that remarkable shade of green. How had he never noticed them before?

"Well, it really depends on the kind of dental surgery, don't you think?" she asked.

Rodolfo couldn't have been more surprised if the quietly officious creature had tossed off her clothes and started dancing on the table—well, there was no need to exaggerate. He'd have summoned the pal-

ace doctors if the princess had done anything of the
kind. After appreciating the show for a moment or
two, of course, because he was a man, not a statue.
But the fact she appeared to be teasing him was as-
tounding, nonetheless.

"A root canal, at the very least," he offered.

"With or without anesthesia?"

"If it was with anesthesia you'd sleep right
through it," Rodolfo pointed out. "Hardly any suffering at all."

"Everyone knows there's no point doing one's
duty unless one can brag forever about the amount
of suffering required to survive the task," the princess said, moving farther into the room. She stopped
and rested her hand on the high, brocaded back of a
chair that had likely cradled the posteriors of kings
dating back to the ninth century, and all Rodolfo
could think was that he wanted her to keep going.
To keep walking toward him. To put herself within
reach so he could—

Calm down, he ordered himself. *Now.* So sternly
he sounded like his father in his own head.

"You are describing martyrdom," he pointed out.

Valentina shot him a smile. "Is there a difference?"

Rodolfo stood still because he didn't quite know
what he might do if he moved. He watched this
woman he'd written off months ago as if he'd never
seen her before. There was something in the way
she walked this afternoon that tugged at him. There
was a new roll to her hips, perhaps. Something he'd

almost call a swagger, assuming a princess of her spotless background and perfect genes was capable of anything so basic and enticing. Still, he couldn't look away as she rounded the settee he'd abandoned and settled herself in its center with a certain delicacy that was at odds with the way she'd moved through the old, spectacularly royal room. Almost as if she was more uncertain than she looked…but that made as little sense as the rest.

"I was reading about you on the plane back from London today," she told him, surprising him all over again.

"And here I thought we were maintaining the polite fiction that you did not sully your royal eyes with the squalid tabloids."

"Ordinarily I would not, of course," she replied, and then her mouth curved. Rodolfo was captivated. And somewhat horrified at that fact. But still captivated, all the same. "It is beneath me, obviously."

He sketched a bow that would have made his grandfather proud. "Obviously."

"I am a princess, not a desperate shopgirl who wants nothing more than to escape her dreary life, and must imagine herself into fantastical stories and half-truths presented as gospel."

"Quite so."

"But I must ask you a question." And on that she smiled again, that same serene curve of her lips that had about put him to sleep before. That was not the effect it had on him today. By a long shot.

"You can ask me anything, princess," Rodolfo heard himself say.

In a lazy, smoky sort of tone he'd never used in her presence before. Because this was the princess he was going to marry, not one of the enterprising women who flung themselves at him everywhere he went, looking for a taste of Europe's favorite daredevil prince.

There was no denying it. Suddenly, out of nowhere, he wanted his future wife.

Desperately.

As if she could tell—as if she'd somehow become the sort of woman who could read a man's desire and use it against him, when he'd have sworn she was anything but—Valentina's smile deepened.

She tilted her head to one side. "It's about your shocking double standard," she said sweetly. "If you can cat your way through all of Europe, why can't I?"

Something black and wild and wholly unfamiliar surged in him then, making Rodolfo's hands curl into fists and his entire body go tense, taut.

Then he really shocked the hell out of himself.

"Because you can't," he all but snarled, and there was no pretending that wasn't exactly what he was doing. *Snarling.* No matter how unlikely. "Like it or not, princess, you are mine."

CHAPTER THREE

PRINCE RODOLFO WAS not what Natalie was expecting.

No picture—and there were thousands, at a conservative estimate, every week he continued to draw breath—could adequately capture the *size* of Europe's favorite royal adrenaline junkie. That was the first thing that struck her. Sure, she'd seen the detailed telephoto shots of his much-hallowed abs as he emerged from various sparkling Mediterranean waters that had dominated whole summers of international swooning. And there was that famous morning he'd spent on a Barcelona balcony one spring, stretching and taking in the sunlight in boxer briefs and nothing else, but somehow all of those revealing pictures had managed to obscure the sheer *size* of the man. He was well over six feet, with hard, strong shoulders that could block out a day or two. And more than that, there was a leashed, humming sort of *power* in the man that photographs of him concealed entirely.

Or, Natalie thought, *maybe he's the one who does the concealing.*

But she couldn't think about what this man might be hiding beneath the surface. Not when the surface itself was so mesmerizing. She still felt as dazed as she'd been when she'd walked in this room and seen him waiting for her, dwarfing the furniture with all that contained physicality as he stood before the grand old fireplace. He looked like an athlete masquerading as a prince, with thick dark hair that was not quite tamed and the sort of dark chocolate eyes that a woman could lose herself in for a lifetime or three. His lean and rangy hard male beauty was packed into black trousers and a soft-looking button-down shirt that strained to handle his biceps and his gloriously sculpted chest. His hands were large and aristocratic at once, his voice was an authoritative rumble that seemed to murmur deep within her and then sink into a bright flame between her legs, his gaze was shockingly direct—and Natalie was not at all prepared. For any of it. For *him*.

She'd expected this real-life Prince Charming to be as repellent as he'd always been in the stories her mother had told her as a child about men just like him. Dull and vapid. Obsessed with something obscure, like hound breeding. Vain and huffy and bland, all the way through. Not...*this*.

Valentina had said that her fiancé was attractive in an offhanded, uncomplimentary way. She'd failed to mention that he was, in fact, upsettingly—almost incomprehensibly—stunning. The millions of fawning, admiring pictures of Crown Prince Rodolfo did not do him any justice, it turned out, and the truth of him took all the air from the room. From Natalie's lungs, for that matter. Her stomach felt scraped hollow as it plummeted to her feet, and then stayed there. But after a moment in the doorway where she'd seen nothing but him and the world had seemed to smudge a little bit around its luxe, literally palatial edges, Natalie had rallied.

It was hard enough trying to walk in the ridiculous shoes she was wearing—with her weight back on her heels, as ordered—and not goggle in slack-jawed astonishment at the palace all around her. *The actual, real live palace.* Valentina had pointed out that Natalie had likely visited remarkable places before, thanks to her job, and that was certainly true. But it was one thing to be treated as a guest in a place like Murin Castle. Or more precisely, as the employee of a guest, however valued by the guest in question. It was something else entirely to be treated as if it was all…hers.

The staff had curtsied and bowed when Natalie had stepped onto the royal jet. The guards had stood at attention. A person who was clearly her personal aide had catered to her during the quick flight, quickly filling her in on the princess's schedule and plans and then leaving her to her own devices. Natalie had spent years doing the exact same thing, so she'd learned a few things about Valentina in the way her efficient staff operated around her look-alike. That she was well liked by those who worked for her, which made Natalie feel oddly warm inside, as if that was some kind of reflection on her instead of the princess. That Valentina was not overly fussy or precious, given the way the staff served her food and acted while they did it. And that she was addicted to romance novels, if the stacks of books with bright-colored covers laid out for her perusal was any indication.

Then, soon enough, the plane had landed on the tiny little jewel of an island nestled in the Mediterranean Sea. Natalie's impressions were scattered as they flew in. Hills stretched high toward the sun, then sloped into the sea, covered in olive groves, tidy red roofs and the soaring arches of bell towers and churches. Blue water gleamed everywhere she looked, and white sand beaches nestled up tight to colorful fishing villages and picturesque marinas. There were cheerful sails in the graceful bay and a great, iconic castle set high on a hill. A perfect postcard of an island.

A dream. Except Natalie was wide-awake, and this was really, truly happening.

"Prince Rodolfo awaits your pleasure, Your Highness," a man she assumed was some kind of high-level butler had informed her when she'd been escorted into the palace itself, with guards saluting her arrival. She'd been too busy trying to look as if the splendor pressing in on her from all sides was so terribly common that she hardly noticed it to do more than nod, in some approximation of the princess's elegant inclination of her head. Then she'd had to follow the same butler through the palace, trying to walk with ease and confidence in shoes she was certain were not meant to be walked in at all, much less down endless marble halls.

She'd expected Prince Rodolfo to be seedier in person than in his photos. Softer of jaw, meaner of eye. And up himself in every possible way. She had not expected to find herself so stunned at the sight of him that she'd had to reach out and hold on to the furniture to keep her knees from giving out beneath her, for the love of all that was holy.

And then he'd spoken, and Natalie had understood—with a certain, sinking feeling that only made that breathlessness worse—that she was in more than a little hot water. It had never crossed her mind that *she* might find this prince—or any prince—attractive. It had never even occurred to her that she might be affected in any way by a man who carried that sort of title or courted the sort of attention Prince Rodolfo did. Natalie had never liked *flashy*. It was always a deliberate distraction, never anything real. Working for one of the most powerful men in the world had made her more than a little jaded when it came to other male displays of supposed strength. She knew what real might look like, how it was maintained and more, how it was wielded. A petty little princeling who liked to fling himself out of airplanes could only be deeply unappealing in person, she'd imagined.

She'd never imagined...*this*.

It was possible her mouth had run away with her, as some kind of defense mechanism.

And then, far more surprising, Prince Rodolfo wasn't the royal dullard she'd been expecting—all party and no substance. The sculpted mouth of his... *did things* to her as he revealed himself to be something a bit more intriguing than the airhead she'd expected. Especially when that look in his dark eyes took a turn toward the feral.

Stop, she ordered herself sternly. *This is another woman's fiancé, no matter what she might think of him.*

Natalie had to order herself to pay attention to what was happening as the Prince's surprisingly possessive words rang through the large room that teemed with antiques and the sort of dour portraits that usually turned out to have been painted by ancient masters, were always worth unconscionable amounts of money and made everyone in them look shriveled and dour. Or more precisely, she had to focus on their conversation, and not the madness that was going on inside her body.

You are mine didn't sound like the kind of thing the man Valentina had described would say. Ever. It didn't sound at all like the man the tabloids drooled over, or all those ex-lovers moaned about in exclusive interviews, mostly to complain about how quickly each and every one of them was replaced with the next.

In fact, unless she was mistaken, His Royal Highness, Prince Rodolfo, he of so many paramours in so many places that there were many internet graphs and user forums dedicated to tracking them all, looked as surprised by that outburst as she was.

"That hardly seems fair, does it?" she asked mildly, hoping he couldn't tell how thrown she was by him. Hoping it would go away if she ignored it. "I don't see why I have to confine myself to only you when you don't feel compelled to limit yourself. In any way at all, according to my research."

"Is there someone you wish to add to your stable, princess?" Rodolfo asked, in a smooth sort of way that was at complete odds with that hard, near-gold gleam in his dark eyes that set off every alarm in her body. Whether she ignored it or not. "Name the lucky gentleman."

"A lady never shares such things," she demurred. Then smiled the way she always had at the officious secretaries of her boss's rivals, all of whom under-estimated her. Once. "Unlike you, Your Highness."

"I cannot help it if the press follows me every-where I go." She sensed more than heard the growl in his voice. He was still standing where he'd been when she arrived, arranged before the immense fire-place like some kind of royal offering, but if he'd thought it made him look idle and at his ease he'd miscalculated. All she could see when she looked at him was how *big* he was. Big and hard and beauti-ful from head to toe and, God help her, she couldn't seem to control her reaction to him. "Just as I cannot keep them from writing any fabrication they desire. They prefer a certain narrative, of course. It sells."

"How tragic. I had no idea you were a misunderstood monk."

"I am a man, princess." He didn't quite bare his teeth. There was no reason at all Natalie should feel the cut of them against her skin. "Were you in some doubt?"

Natalie reminded herself that she, personally, had no stake in this. No matter how many stories her mother had told her about men like him and the careless way they lived their lives. No matter that Prince Rodolfo proved that her mother was right every time he swam with sharks or leaped from planes or trekked for a month in remotest Patagonia with no access to the outside world or thought to his country should he never return. And no matter the way her heart was kicking at her and her breath seemed to tangle in her throat. This wasn't about *her* at all.

I'm going to sort out your fiancé as a little wedding gift to you, she'd texted Valentina when she'd recovered from her shell shock and had emerged from the fateful bathroom in London to watch Achilles Casilieris's plane launch itself into the air without her. The beauty of the other princess having taken her bag when she'd left—with Natalie's phone inside it—was that Natalie knew her own number and could reach the woman who was inhabiting her life. You're welcome.

Good luck with that, Valentina had responded. He's unsortable. Deliberately, I imagine.

As far as Natalie was concerned, that was permission to come on in, guns blazing. She had nothing to lose by saying the things Valentina wouldn't. And there was absolutely no reason she should feel that hot, intent look he was giving her low and tight in her belly. No reason at all.

She made a show of looking around the vast room the scrupulously correct butler who had ushered her here had called a *parlor* in ringing tones. She'd had to work hard not to seem cowed, by the butler or the scale of the private wing he'd led her through, all dizzying chandeliers and astoundingly beautiful rooms clogged with priceless antiques and jaw-dropping art.

"I don't see any press here," she said, instead of debating his masculinity. For God's sake.

"Obviously not." Was it her imagination or did Rodolfo sound a little less…civilized? "We are on palace grounds. Your father would have them whipped."

"If you wanted to avoid the press, you could," Natalie pointed out. With all the authority of a person who had spent five years keeping Achilles Casilieris out of the press's meaty claws. "You don't."

Was it possible this mighty, beautiful prince looked…ill at ease? If only for a moment?

"I never promised you that I would declaw myself, Valentina," he said, and it took Natalie a moment to remember why he was calling her Valentina. Because that's who he thought she was, of course. Princess Valentina, who had to marry him in two months. Not mouthy, distressingly common Natalie, who was unlikely to marry anyone since she spent her entire life embroiled in and catering to the needs of a man who likely wouldn't be able to pick her out of a lineup. "I told you I would consider it after the wedding. For a time."

Natalie shrugged, and told herself there was no call for her to feel slapped down by his response. He wasn't going to marry *her*. She certainly didn't need to feel wounded by the way he planned to run his relationship. Critical, certainly. But not *wounded*.

"As will I," she said mildly.

Rodolfo studied her for a long moment, and Natalie forced herself to hold that seething dark glare while he did it. She even smiled and settled back against the delicate little couch, as if she was utterly relaxed. When she was nothing even remotely like it.

"No," he said after a long, long time, his voice dark and lazy and something else she felt more than heard. "I think not."

Natalie held back the little shiver that threatened her then, because she knew, somehow, that he would see it and leap to the worst possible conclusion.

"You mistake me," she said coolly. "I wasn't asking your permission. I was stating a fact."

"I would suggest that you think very carefully about acting on this little scheme of yours, princess,"

Rodolfo said in that same dark, stirring tone. "You will not care for my response, I am certain."

Natalie crossed her legs and forced herself to relax even more against the back of her little couch. Well. To look it, anyway. As if she had never been more at her ease, despite the drumming of her pulse.

She waved a hand the way Valentina had done in London, so nonchalantly. "Respond however you wish. You have my blessing."

He laughed, then. The sound was rougher than Natalie would have imagined a royal prince's laugh ought to have been, and silkier than she wanted to admit as it wrapped itself around her. And all of that was a far second to the way amusement danced over his sculpted, elegant face, making him look not only big and surprisingly powerful, but very nearly approachable. Magnetic, even.

Something a whole lot more than magnetic. It lodged itself inside of her, then glowed.

Good lord, Natalie thought in another sort of daze as she gazed back at him. *This is the most dangerous man I've ever met.*

"I take it this is an academic discussion," Rodolfo said when he was finished laughing like that and using up all the light in the world, so cavalierly. "I had no idea you felt so strongly about what I did or didn't do, much less with whom. I had no idea you cared what I did at all. In fact, princess, I wasn't certain you heard a single word I've uttered in your presence in all these months."

He moved from the grand fireplace then, and watching him in motion was not exactly an improvement. Or it was a significant improvement, depending on how she looked at it. He was sleek for such a big man, and moved far too smoothly toward the slightly more substantial chair at a diagonal to where Natalie sat. He tossed himself into the stunningly wrought antique with a carelessness that should have snapped it into kindling, but didn't.

It occurred to her that he was far more aware of himself and his power than he appeared. That he was something of an iceberg, showing only the slightest bit of himself and containing multitudes beneath the surface. She didn't want to believe it. She wanted him to be a vapid, repellant playboy who she could slap into place during her time as a make-believe princess. But there was that assessing gleam in his dark gaze that told her that whatever else this prince was, he wasn't the least bit vapid.

And was rather too genuinely *charming* for her peace of mind, come to that.

He settled in his chair and stretched out his long, muscled legs so that they *almost* brushed hers, then smiled.

Natalie kept her own legs where they were, because shifting away from him would show a weakness she refused to let him see. She refused, as if her life depended on that refusal, and she didn't much care for the hysterical notion that it really, truly did.

"I don't care at all what you do or don't do," she

assured him. "But it certainly appears that you can't say the same, for some reason."

"I am not the one who started making proclamations about my sexual intentions. I think you'll find that was you. Here. Today." That curve of his mouth deepened. "Entirely unprovoked."

"My mistake. Because a man who has grown up manipulating the press in no way sends a distinct message when he spends the bulk of his very public engagement 'escorting' other women to various events."

His gaze grew warmer, and that sculpted mouth curved. "I am a popular man."

"What I am suggesting to you is that you are not the only popular person in this arrangement. I'm baffled at your Neanderthal-like response to a simple statement of fact, when you have otherwise been at such pains to present yourself as the very image of modernity in royal affairs."

"We are sitting in an ancient castle on an island with a history that rivals Athens itself, discussing our upcoming marriage, which is the cold-blooded intermingling of two revered family lines for wealth and power, exactly as it might have been were we conducting this conversation in the Parthenon." His dark brows rose. "What part of this did you find particularly modern?"

"The two of us, I thought, before I walked in this room." She smiled brightly and let her foot dangle a bit too close to his leg. As if she didn't care at all that he was encroaching into her personal space. As if the idea of even so innocuous a touch did nothing at all to her central nervous system. As if he were not the sort of man she'd hated all her life, on principle. *And as if he were not promised to another,* she snapped at herself in disgust, but still, she didn't retreat the way she should have. In case she was wondering what kind of person she was. "Now I suspect the Social Media Prince is significantly more caveman-like than he wants his millions of adoring followers to realize."

"I am the very soul of a Renaissance man, I assure you. I am merely aware of what the public will and will not support and I hate to break it you, princess, but the tabloids are not as forgiving of royal indiscretions as you appear to be."

"You surprise me again, Your Highness. I felt certain that a man in your position could not possibly care what the tabloid hacks did or did not forgive, given how much material you give them to work with. Daily."

"The two of us can sit in this room and bask in our progressive values, I am sure," Rodolfo murmured, and the look in his dark eyes did not strike Natalie as particularly progressive. "But public sentiment, I think you will find, is distressingly traditional. People may enjoy any number of their own extramarital affairs. It doesn't make them tolerant when a supposed fairy-tale princess strays from her charmed life. If anything, it makes the stones they cast heavier and more pointed."

"So, to unpack that, you personally wish to carry on as if we are single and free, but are prevented from following your heart's desire because you suddenly fear public perception?" She eyed him balefully and made no attempt to hide it. "That's a bit hard to believe, coming from the man who told me not twenty minutes ago that he refused to be *declawed.*"

"You are not this naive, princess." And the look he gave her then seemed to prickle along her skin, lighting fires Natalie was terribly afraid would never go out. "You know perfectly well that I can do as I like with only minimal repercussions. It is you who cannot. You have built an entire life on your spotless character. What would happen were you to be revealed as nothing more or less than a creature as human as the rest of us?"

CHAPTER FOUR

RODOLFO HAD LONG ceased recognizing himself. And yet he kept talking.

"It will be difficult to maintain the fiction that you are a saint if your lovers are paraded through the tabloids of Europe every week," he pointed out, as if he didn't care one way or the other.

Somehow, he had the sense that the confounding woman who sat close enough to tempt him near to madness knew better. He could see it in the way her green eyes gleamed as she watched him. She was lounging in the settee as if it was a makeshift throne and she was already queen. And now she waved a languid hand, calling attention to her fine bones and the elegant fingers Rodolfo wanted all over his body. Rather desperately.

"It is you who prefer to ignore discretion," she said lightly enough. "I assume you get something out of the spotlight you shine so determinedly into your bedroom. I must congratulate you, as it is not every man who would be able to consistently perform with such an audience, so many years past his prime."

"I beg your pardon. Did you just question my… performance?"

"No need to rile yourself, Your Highness. The entire world has seen more than enough of your prowess. I'm sure you are marvelously endowed with the—ah—necessary tools."

It took Rodolfo a stunned moment to register that the sensation moving in him then was nothing short of sheer astonishment. Somewhere between temper and laughter and yet neither at once.

"Let me make sure I am following this extraordinary line of thought," he began, trying to keep himself under control somehow—something that he could not recall ever being much of an issue before. Not with Princess Valentina, certainly. Not with any other woman he'd ever met.

"Whether or not it is extraordinary is between you and your revolving selection of aspiring hyphenates, I would think." When he could only stare blankly at her, she carried on almost merrily. "Model slash actress slash waitress slash air hostess, whatever the case may be. You exchange one for another so quickly, it's hard to keep track."

"I feel as if I've toppled off the side of the planet into an alternate reality," Rodolfo said then, after a moment spent attempting to digest what she'd said. What she'd actually dared say directly to his face. "Wherein Princess Valentina of Murin is sitting in my presence issuing veiled insults about my sexual performance and, indeed, my manhood itself."

"In this reality, we do not use the word *manhood* when we mean penis," Princess Valentina said with the same serene smile she'd always worn, back when he'd imagined she was boring. He couldn't understand how he'd misread her so completely. "It's a bit missish, isn't it?"

"What I cannot figure out is what you hope to gain from poking at me, Valentina," he said softly. "I am not given to displays of temper, if that is what you hoped. Perhaps you forgot that I subject myself to extreme stress often. For fun. It is very, very difficult to get under my skin."

She smiled with entirely too much satisfaction for his comfort. "Says the man who had a rather strong reaction to the idea that what he feels constitutes reasonable behavior for him might also be equally appropriate for his fiancée."

"I assume you already recognize that there is no stopping the train we're on," he continued in the same quiet way, because it was that or give in to the simmering thing that was rumbling around inside of him, making him feel more precarious than he had in a long, long time. "The only way to avoid this marriage is to willfully cause a crisis in two kingdoms, and to what end? To make a point about free will? That is a lovely sentiment, I am sure, but it is not for you or me. We are not free. We belong to our countries and the people we serve. I would expect a woman whose very name is synonymous with her duty to understand that."

"That is a curious statement indeed from the only heir to an ancient throne who spends the bulk of his leisure time courting his own death." She let that land, that curve to her lips but nothing like a smile in her direct green stare. And she wasn't done. "Very much as if he was under the impression he did, in fact, owe nothing to his country at all."

Rodolfo's jaw felt like granite. "I can only assume that you are a jealous little thing, desperate to hide what you really want behind all these halfhearted feints and childish games."

The princess laughed. It was a smoky sound that felt entirely too much like a caress. "Why am I not surprised that so conceited a man would achieve that conclusion so quickly? Alas, I am hiding nothing, Your Highness."

He felt his lips curl in something much too fierce to be polite. "If you want to know whether or not I am marvelously endowed, princess, you need only ask for a demonstration."

She rolled her eyes, and perhaps that was what did it. Rodolfo was not used to being dismissed by beautiful women. Quite the contrary, they trailed around after him, begging for the scraps of his attention. He'd become adept at handling them before he'd left his teens. The ones who pretended to dislike him to get his attention, the ones who propositioned him straight out, the ones who acted as if they were shy, the ones so overcome and starstruck they stammered or wept or could only stare in silence. He'd seen it all.

But he had no way to process what was happening here with this woman he'd dismissed as uninteresting and uninterested within moments of their meeting as adults last fall. He had no idea what to do with a woman who set him on fire from across a room, and then treated him like a somewhat sad and boring joke.

He could handle just about anything, he realized, save indifference.

Rodolfo simply reached over and picked the princess up from the settee, hauling her through the air and setting her across his lap.

It was not a smart move. At best it was a test of that indifference she was flinging around the palace so casually, but it still wasn't smart.

But Rodolfo found he didn't give a damn.

The princess's porcelain cheeks flushed red and hot. She was a soft, slight weight against him, but his entire body exulted in the feel of her. Her scent was something so prosaic it hit him as almost shockingly exotic—soap. That was all. Her hands came up to brace against his chest, her copper hair was a silky shower over his arm and she was breathing hard and fast, making her exactly as much of a liar as he'd imagined she was.

She was many things, his hidden gem of a princess bride, but she was not *indifferent* to him. It felt like a victory.

"Do you think I cannot read women?" he asked her, his face temptingly, deliciously close to hers.

Her gaze was defiant. "There has long been debate about whether or not you can read anything else."

"I know you want me, princess. I can see it. I can feel it. The pulse in your throat, the look in your eyes. The way you tremble against me."

"That is sheer amazement that you think you can manhandle me this way, nothing more."

He moved the arm that wasn't wrapped around her back, sliding his hand to the delectable bit of thigh that was bared beneath the hem of her dress and just held it there. Her skin was a revelation, warm and soft. And her perfect, aristocratic oval of a face was tipped back, his for the taking.

Maybe he was the Neanderthal she'd claimed he was, after all. For the first time in his life, he felt as if he was that and more. A beast in every possible way, inside and out.

"What would happen if I slid my hand up under your skirt?" he asked her, bending even closer, so his mouth was a mere breath from hers.

"I would summon the royal guard and have you cast into the dungeons, the more medieval the better."

He ignored that breathy, insubstantial threat, along with the oddity of the Princess of Murin talking of dungeons in a palace that had never had any in the whole of its storied history. He concentrated on her body instead.

"What would I find, princess? How wet are you? How much of a liar will your body prove you to be?"

"Unlike you," she whispered fiercely, "I don't feel

the need to prove myself in a thousand different sexual arenas."

But she didn't pull away. He noted that she didn't even try.

"You don't need to concern yourself with any arena but this one," he said, gruff against her mouth and his palm still full of her soft flesh. "And you need not prove yourself to anyone but me."

Rodolfo had kissed her once before. It had been a bloodless, mechanical photo op on the steps of Murin Castle. They had held hands and beamed insincerely at the crowds, and then he had pressed a chaste, polite sort of closemouthed kiss against her mouth to seal the deal. No muss, no fuss. It hadn't been unpleasant in any way. But there hadn't been anything to it. No fire. No raw, aching need. Rodolfo had experienced more intense handshakes.

That was not the way he kissed her today. Because everything was different, somehow. Himself included.

He didn't bother with any polite, bloodless kiss. Rodolfo took her mouth as if he owned it. As if there was nothing *arranged* about the two of them and never had been. As if he'd spent the night inside her, making her his in every possible way, and couldn't contain himself another moment.

Her taste flooded his senses, making him glad on some distant level that he'd had the accidental foresight to remain seated, because otherwise he thought she might have knocked him off his feet. He opened his mouth over hers, angling his jaw to revel in the slick, hot fit.

She was a marvel. And she was his, whether she liked it or not. No matter what inflammatory thing she said to rile him up or insult him into an international incident that would shame them both, or whatever the hell she was doing. How had he thought otherwise for even a moment?

Rodolfo lost his mind.

And his lovely bride-to-be did not push him off or slap his face. She didn't lie there in icy indifference. Oh, no.

She surged against him, wrapping her arms around his neck to pull him closer, and she kissed him back. Again and again and again.

For a moment there was nothing but that fire that roared between them. Wild. Insane. Unchecked and unmanageable.

And then in the next moment, she was shoving away from him. She twisted to pull herself from his grasp and then clambered off his lap, and he let her. Of course he bloody let her, and no matter the state of him as she went. That it was a new state—one he'd never experienced before, having about as much experience with frustrated desire as he did with governing the country he would one day rule—was something he kept to himself. Mostly because he hardly knew what to make of it.

The princess looked distressed as she threw herself across the room and away from him. She was trembling as she caught herself against the carved edge of the stone fireplace, and then she took a deep, long breath. To settle herself, perhaps, if she felt even a fraction of the things he did. Or perhaps she merely needed to steady herself in those shoes.

"Valentina," he began, but her name seemed to hit her like a slap. She stiffened, then held up a hand as if to silence him. Yet another new experience.

And he could still taste her in his mouth. His body was still clamoring for her touch. He wanted her, desperately, so he let her quiet him like an errant schoolboy instead of the heir to an ancient throne.

"That must never happen again," she said with soft, intense sincerity, her gaze fixed on the fireplace, where an exultant flower arrangement took the place of the fires that had crackled there in the colder months.

"Come now, princess." He didn't sound like himself. Gruff. Low. "I think you know full well it must. We will make heirs, you and I. It is the primary purpose of our union."

She stood taller, then turned to face him, and he was struck by what looked like *torment* on her face. As if this was hard for her, whatever the hell was happening here, which made no sense. This had always been her destiny. If not with Rodolfo, then with some other Crown-sanctioned suitor. The woman he'd thought he'd known all these months had always seemed, if not precisely thrilled by the prospect, resigned to it. He imagined the change in her would have been fascinating if he wasn't half-blind from *wanting* her so badly.

"No," she said, and he was struck again by how different her voice sounded. But how could that be? He shook that off and concentrated instead on what she'd said.

"You must be aware that there can be no negotiation on this point." He tamped down on the terrible need making his body over into a stranger's, and concentrated instead on reality.

She frowned at him. "What if we can't produce heirs? It's more common than you think."

"And covered at some length in the contracts we signed," he agreed, trying to rein in his impatience. "But we must try, Valentina. It is part of our agreement." He shook his head when she started to speak. "If you plan to tell me that this is medieval, you are correct. It is. Literally. The same provisions have covered every such marriage between people like us since the dawn of time. You cannot have imagined that a royal wedding at our rank would allow for anything else, can you?"

Something he would have called fierce inhabited her face for a moment, and then was gone.

"You misunderstand me." She ran her hands down the front of her dress as if it needed smoothing, but all Rodolfo could think of was the feel of her in his arms and the soft skin of her thigh against his palm. "I have every intention of doing my duty, Your Highness. But I will only be as faithful to you as you are to me."

He shook his head. "I am not a man who backs down from a challenge, princess. You must know this."

"It's not a challenge." Her gaze was dark when it met his. "It's a fact. As long as you ignore your commitments, I'll do the same. What have I got to lose? I'll always know that our children are mine. Let's hope you can say the same."

And on that note—while he remained frozen in his chair, stunned that she would dare threaten him openly with such a thing—Rodolfo's suddenly fascinating princess pulled herself upright and then swept out of the room.

He let her go.

It was clear to him after today that not only did he need to get to know his fiancée a whole lot better than he had so far, he needed to up his game overall where she was concerned. And when it came to games, Rodolfo had the advantage, he knew.

Because he'd never, ever lost a single game he'd ever played.

His princess was not going to be the first.

It was difficult to make a dramatic exit when Natalie had no idea where she was going.

She was on her third wrong turn—and on the verge of frustrated tears—when she hailed a confused-looking maid who, after a stilted conversation in which Natalie tried not to sound as if she was lost in what should have been her home, led her off into a completely different part of the palace and into what were clearly Valentina's own private rooms. Though "rooms" was an understated way to put it. The series of vast, exquisitely furnished chambers were more like a lavish, sprawling penthouse contained in the palace and sporting among its many rooms a formal dining area, a fully equipped media center and a vast bedroom suite complete with a wide balcony that looked off toward the sea and a series of individual rooms that together formed the princess's wardrobe. The shoe room alone was larger than the flat Natalie kept on the outskirts of London, yet barely used, thanks to her job.

Staff bustled about in the outer areas of the large suite, presumably adhering to the princess's usual schedule, but the bedroom was blessedly empty. It was there that Natalie found a surprisingly comfortable chaise, curled herself up on it with a sigh of something not quite relief and finally gave herself leave to contemplate the sort of person she'd discovered she was today.

It left a bitter taste in her mouth.

She'd always harbored a secret fantasy that should she ever stumble over a Prince Charming type—and not be forced into studied courtesy because she represented her employer—she'd shred him to pieces. Because even if the man in question wasn't the one who'd taught her mother to be so bitter, it was a fair bet that he'd ruined someone else's life. That was what Prince Charmings *did*. Even in the fairy tale, the man had left a trail of mutilated feet and broken families behind him everywhere he went. Natalie had been certain she could slap an overconfident ass like that down without even trying very hard.

And instead, she'd kissed him.

Oh, she tried to pretend otherwise. She tried to muster up a little outrage at the way Rodolfo had put his hands on her and hauled her onto his lap—but what did any of that matter? He hadn't held her there against her will. She could have stood up at any time.

She hadn't. Quite the contrary.

And when his mouth had touched hers, she'd *imploded.*

Not only had Natalie kissed the kind of man she'd always hated on principle, but she'd kissed one promised to another woman. If that wasn't enough, she'd threatened to marry him and then present him with children that weren't his. As punishment? Just to be cruel? She had no idea. She only knew that her mouth had opened and out the threat had come.

The worst part was, she'd seen that stunned, furious look on the Prince's face when she'd issued that threat. Natalie had no doubt that he believed that she would do exactly that. Worse, that *Princess Valentina* was the sort of person who, apparently, thought nothing of that kind of behavior.

"Great," she muttered out loud, to the soft chaise beneath her and the soothing landscapes on the walls. "You've made everything worse."

It was one thing to try to make things better for

Valentina, who Natalie imagined was having no fun at all contending with the uncertain temper of Mr. Casilieris. Natalie was used to fixing things. That was what she did with her life—she sorted things out to be easier, smoother, better for others. But Rodolfo hadn't been as easily managed as she'd expected him to be, and the truth was, she'd never quite recovered from that first, shocking sight of him.

There was a possibility, Natalie acknowledged as she remained curled up on a posh chaise in a princess's bedroom like the sort of soft creature she'd never been, that she still hadn't recovered. *And that you never will,* chimed in a voice from deep inside her, but she dismissed it as unnecessarily dire.

Her clutch—Valentina's clutch—had been delivered here while she'd been off falling for Prince Charming like a ninny, sitting on an engaged man's lap as if she had no spine or will of her own, and making horrible threats about potential royal heirs in line to a throne. Was that treason in a kingdom like Murin? In Tissely? She didn't even know.

"And maybe you should find out before you cause a war," she snapped at herself.

What she did know was that she didn't recognize herself, all dressed up in another woman's castle as if that life could ever fit her. And she didn't like it.

Natalie pushed up off the chaise and went to sweep up the clutch from where it had been left on the padded bench that claimed the real estate at the foot of the great four-poster bed. She'd examined the contents on the plane, fascinated. Princesses apparently carried very little, unlike personal assistants, who could live out of their shoulder bags for weeks in a pinch. There was no money or identification, likely because neither was necessary when you had access to an entire treasury filled with currency stamped with your own face. Valentina carried only her mobile, a tube of extremely high-end lip gloss and a small compact mirror.

Natalie sat on the bench with Valentina's mobile in her hand and looked around the quietly elegant bedroom, though she hardly saw it. The adrenaline of the initial switch had given way to sheer anxiety once she'd arrived in Murin. She'd expected to be called out at any moment and forced to explain how and why she was impersonating the princess. But no one had blinked, not even Prince Rodolfo.

Maybe she shouldn't be surprised that now that she was finally alone, she felt a little lost. Maybe that was the price anyone could expect to pay when swapping identities with a complete stranger. Especially one who happened to be a royal princess to boot.

It was times like this that Natalie wished she had the sort of relationship with her mother that other people seemed to have with theirs. She'd like nothing more than to call Erica up and ask for some advice, or maybe just so she could feel soothed, somehow, by the fact of her mother's existence. But that had never been the way her mother operated. Erica had liked Natalie best when she was a prop. The pretty little girl she could trot out when it suited her, to tug on a heartstring or to prove that she was maternal when, of course, she wasn't. Not really. Not beyond the telling of the odd fairy tale with a grim ending, which Natalie had learned pretty early on was less for her than for her mother.

No wonder Natalie had lost herself in school. It didn't matter where they moved. It didn't matter what was going on in whatever place Erica was calling home that month. Natalie could always count on her studies. Whether she was behind the class or ahead of it when she showed up as the new kid, who cared? School always gave her a project of one sort or another. She'd viewed getting into college—on a full academic scholarship, of course, because Erica had laughed when Natalie had asked if there would be any parental contributions to her education and then launched into another long story about the evils of rich, selfish men—as her escape. College had been four years of an actual place to call home, at last. Plus classes. Basically nirvana, as far as Natalie had been concerned.

But that kind of overachieving behavior, while perfect for her eventual career as the type A assistant to the most picky and overbearing man alive, had not exactly helped Natalie make any friends. She'd always been the new kid in whatever school she'd ended up in. Then, while she wasn't the new kid at college, she was so used to her usual routine of studying constantly that she hadn't known how to stop it. She and her freshman-year roommate had gotten along well enough and they'd even had lunch a few times over the next few years, all very pleasant, but it hadn't ever bloomed into the sort of friendships Natalie knew other women had. She'd had a boyfriend her junior year, which had been more exciting in theory than in fact. And then she'd started working for Mr. Casilieris after graduation and there hadn't been time for anything but him, ever again.

All of this had been perfectly fine with her yesterday. She'd been proud of her achievements and the fact no one had helped her in equal measure. Well. She'd wanted to quit her job, but surely that was a reasonable response to five years of Achilles Casilieris. And today, sitting on the cushioned bench at the foot of a princess's bed with a medieval castle looming all around her like an accusation, it was clear to Natalie that really, she could have used someone to call.

Anyone except the person she knew she had to call, that was.

But Natalie hadn't dealt with a terrifying man like Achilles Casilieris for years by being a coward, no matter how tempting it was to become one now. She blew out a breath, then dialed her own mobile number. She knew that the flight she should have been on right now, en route to New York City, hadn't landed yet. She even knew that all the calls she'd set up would likely have ended—but she wasn't surprised when Valentina didn't answer. Mr. Casilieris was likely tearing strips out of the princess's hide, because no matter how she'd handled the situation, it wouldn't have been to his satisfaction. She was a bit surprised that Valentina hadn't confessed all and that the Casilieris plane wasn't landing in Murin right now to discharge her—and so Achilles Casilieris could fire Natalie in person for deceiving him.

Really, it hadn't been nice of Natalie to let Valentina take her place. She'd known what the other woman was walking into. God help the poor princess if she failed to provide Mr. Casilieris with what he wanted three seconds before he knew he wanted it. When she'd started, Achilles Casilieris had been famous for cycling through assistants in a matter of hours, sometimes, depending on the foulness of his mood. Everyone was an idiot, as he was all too happy to make clear, especially the people he paid to assist him. Everyone fell short of his impossibly high standards. If he thought Natalie had lost her ability to do her job the way he liked it done, he'd fire her without a second thought. She'd never been in any doubt about that.

Which meant that really, she should have been a little more concerned about the job Valentina was almost certainly botching up right this very minute, somewhere high above the Atlantic Ocean.

But she found she couldn't work up the usual worry over that eventuality. If he fired her, he fired her. It saved her having to quit, didn't it? And when she tried to stress out about losing the position she'd worked so hard to keep all these years, all she could think of instead was the fact he hadn't known Valentina wasn't her in that bathroom. That despite spending more time with Natalie than with his last ten mistresses combined, he'd failed to recognize her. And meanwhile, Rodolfo had looked at *her*. As if he wanted to climb inside of her. As if he could never, ever get enough. And that mouth of his was sculpted and wicked, knowing and hot...

She heard her own voice asking for a message and a phone number on the other end of the line, but she didn't leave a voice mail at the beep. What would she say? Where would she start? Would she jump right into the kissing and claims that she'd sleep her way around Europe in payback for any extramarital adventures Prince Rodolfo might have? She could hardly believe she'd done either of those things, much less think of how best to tell someone else that she had. Particularly when the someone else was the woman who was expected to marry the man in question.

The fact was, she had no idea what Valentina expected from her arranged marriage. A dry tone in a bathroom to a stranger when discussing her fiancé wasn't exactly a peek into the woman's thoughts on what happily-ever-after looked like for her. Maybe she'd been fine with the expected cheating, like half of Europe seemed to be. Maybe she hadn't cared either way. Natalie had no way to tell.

But it didn't matter what Valentina's position on

any of this was. It didn't make Natalie any happier
with herself that she was hoping, somewhere in there,
that Valentina might give her blessing. Or her forgive-
ness, anyway. And it wasn't as if she could blame the
Prince, either. Prince Rodolfo thought she *was* Valentina. His behavior was completely acceptable. He'd
had every reason to believe he was with his betrothed.

Natalie was the one who'd let another woman's
fiancé kiss her. So thoroughly her breasts still ached
and her lips felt vulnerable and she felt a fist of pure
need clench tight between her legs at the memory.
Natalie was the one who'd kissed him back.

There was no prettying that up. *That* was who
she was.

Natalie put the phone aside, then jumped when
it beeped at her. She snatched it back up, hoping it
was Valentina so she could at least unburden her
conscience—another indication that she was not really the good person she'd always imagined herself to
be, she was well aware—but it was a reminder from
the princess's calendar, telling her she had a dinner
with the king in a few hours.

She wanted to curl back up on that chaise and cry
for a while. Perhaps a week or so. She wanted to look
around for the computer she was sure the princess
must have secreted away somewhere and see if she
could track her actual life as it occurred across the
planet. She wanted to rewind to London and her decision to do this insane thing in the first place and
then think better of pulling such a stunt.

But she swallowed hard as she looked down at that reminder on the mobile screen. *The king.*

All those things she didn't want to think about flooded her then.

If Erica had shortened her name... If all that moving around had been less *wanderer's soul a*nd more *on the run...* If there was really, truly only one reasonable explanation as to how a royal princess and a glorified secretary could pass for each other and it had nothing to do with that tired old saying that *everyone had a twin somewhere...*

If all of those things were true, then the King of Murin—with whom she was about to have a meal—wasn't simply the monarch of this tiny little island kingdom, well-known for his vast personal wealth, many rumors of secret affairs with the world's most glamorous women and the glittering, celebrity-studded life he lived as the head of a tiny, wealthy country renowned for its yacht-friendly harbors and friendly taxes.

He was also very likely her father.

And that was the lure, it turned out, that Natalie couldn't resist.

CHAPTER FIVE

A LITTLE OVER a week later, Natalie thought she might actually be getting the hang of this princess thing. Or settling into her role well enough that she no longer had to mystify the palace staff with odd requests that they lead her to places she should have been able to find on her own.

She'd survived that first dinner with the king, who might or might not have been her father. The truth was, she couldn't tell. If she'd been expecting a mystical, magical sort of reunion, complete with swelling emotions and dazed recognition on both sides, she'd been bitterly disappointed. She'd been led to what was clearly her seat at one end of a long, polished table in what looked like an excruciatingly formal dining room to her but was more likely the king's private, casual eating area given that it was located in his private wing of the palace. She'd stood there for a moment, not knowing what she was supposed to do next. Sit? Wait? Prepare to curtsy?

The doors had been tossed open and a man had strode in with great pomp and circumstance. Even if she hadn't recognized him from the pictures she'd studied online and the portraits littering the castle, Natalie would have known who he was. King Geoffrey of Murin didn't exude the sort of leashed, simmering power Rodolfo did, she couldn't help thinking. He wasn't as magnificently built, for one thing. He was a tall, elegantly slender man who would have looked a bit like an accountant if the suit he wore hadn't so obviously been a bespoke masterpiece and if he hadn't moved with a sort of bone-deep imperiousness that shouted out his identity with each step. It was as if he expected marble floors to form themselves beneath his foot in anticipation that he might place it there. And they did.

"Hello," she'd said when he approached the head of the table, with perhaps a little too much *meaning* in those two syllables. She'd swallowed. Hard.

And the king had paused. Natalie had tensed, her stomach twisting in on itself. *This is it,* she'd thought. *This is the moment you'll not only be exposed as not being Valentina, but recognized as his long-lost daughter—*

"Are you well?" That was it. That was all he'd asked, with a vaguely quizzical look aimed her way.

"Ah, yes." She cleared her throat, though it didn't need clearing. It was her head that had felt dizzy. "Quite well. Thank you. And you?"

"I hope this is not an example of the sort of witty repartee you practice upon Prince Rodolfo," was what Geoffrey had said. He'd nodded at her, which

Natalie had taken as her cue to sit, and then he'd settled himself in his own chair. Only then did he lift
a royal eyebrow and summon the hovering servants
to attend them.

"Not at all," Natalie had managed to reply. And
then some demon had taken her over, and she didn't
stop there. "A future king looks for many things in
a prospective bride, I imagine, from her bloodlines
to whether or not she is reasonably photogenic in all
the necessary pictures. But certainly not wit. That
sort of thing is better saved for the peasants, who require more entertainment to make it through their
dreary lives."

"Very droll, I am sure." The king's eyes were the
same as hers. The same shape, the same unusual
green. And showed the same banked temper she'd
felt in her own too many times to count. A kind of
panicked flush had rolled over her, making her want
to get up and run from the room even as her legs
felt too numb to hold her upright. "I trust you know
better than to make such an undignified display of
inappropriate humor in front of the prince? He may
be deep in a regrettable phase with all those stunts
he pulls, but I assure you, at the end of the day he
is no different from any other man in his position.
Whatever issues he may have with his father now, he
will sooner or later ascend the throne of Tissely. And
when he does, he will not want a comedienne at his
side, Valentina. He will require a queen."

Natalie was used to Achilles Casilieris's version

of slap downs. They were quicker. Louder. He blazed into a fury and then he was done. This was entirely different. This was less a slap down and more a deliberate *pressing down,* putting Natalie firmly and ruthlessly in her place.

She'd found she didn't much care for the experience. Or the place Valentina was apparently expected to occupy.

"But you have no queen," she'd blurted out. Then instantly regretted it when Geoffrey had gazed at her in amazement over his first course. "Sir."

"I do not appreciate this sort of acting out at my table, Valentina," he'd told her, with a certain quiet yet ringing tone. "You know what is expected of you. You were promised to the Tisselians when I still believed I might have more children, or you would take the throne of Murin yourself. But we are Murinese and we do not back out of our promises. If you are finding your engagement problematic, I suggest you either find a way to solve it to your satisfaction or come to a place of peace with its realities. Those are your only choices."

"Was that your choice?" she'd asked.

Maybe her voice had sounded different then. Maybe she'd slipped and let a little emotion in. Natalie hadn't known. What she'd been entirely too clear on was that this man should have recognized her. At the very least, he should have known she wasn't the daughter he was used to seeing at his table. And surely the king knew that he'd had twins. He should have had some kind of inkling that it was *possible* he'd run into his other daughter someday.

And yet if King Geoffrey of Murin noticed that his daughter was any different than usual, he kept it to himself. In the same way that if he was racked nightly by guilt because he'd clearly misplaced a twin daughter some twenty-seven years ago, it did not mar his royal visage in any way.

"We must all make choices," he'd said coolly. "And when we are of the Royal House of Murin, each and every one of those choices must benefit the kingdom. You know this full well and always have. I suggest you resign yourself to your fate, and more gracefully."

And it was the only answer he'd given.

He'd shifted the conversation then, taking charge in what Natalie assumed was his usual way. And he'd talked about nothing much, in more than one language, which would have made Natalie terrified that she'd give herself away, but he hadn't seemed to want much in the way of answers. In Italian, French, or English.

Clearly, the princess's role was to sit quietly and listen as the king expounded on whatever topic he liked. And not to ask questions. No wonder she'd wanted a break.

I have a confession to make, Natalie had texted Valentina later that first night. She'd been back in the princess's absurdly comfortable and elegant bedroom, completely unable to sleep as her conscience was keeping her wide awake.

Confession is good for the soul, I'm reliably informed, Valentina had replied after a moment or two. Natalie had tried to imagine where she might be. In the small room in Mr. Casilieris's vast New York penthouse she thought of as hers? Trying to catch up on work in the office suite on the lower floor? I've never had the pleasure of a life that required a confession. But you can tell me anything.

Natalie had to order herself to stop thinking about her real life, and to start paying attention to Valentina's life, which she was messing up left and right.

Rodolfo kissed me. There. Three quick words, then the send button, and she was no longer keeping a terrible secret to herself.

That time, the pause had seemed to take years.

That sounds a bit more like a confession Rodolfo ought to be making. Though I suppose he wouldn't know one was necessary, would he?

In the spirit of total honesty, Natalie had typed resolutely, because there was nothing to be gained by lying at that point and besides, she clearly couldn't live with herself if she didn't share all of this with Valentina no matter the consequences, I kissed him back.

She'd been sitting up against the headboard then, staring at the phone in her hand with her knees pulled up beneath her chin. She'd expected anger, at the very least. A denunciation or two. And she'd had no idea what that would even look like, coming from a royal princess—would guards burst through the bedroom doors and haul her away? Would Valentina declare her an imposter and have her carried off in chains? Anything seemed possible. Likely, even, given how grievously Natalie had slipped up.

If she'd been a nail-biter, Natalie would have gnawed hers right off. Instead, she tried to make herself breathe.

Someone should, I suppose, Valentina had texted back, after another pause that seemed to last forever and then some. I've certainly never touched him.

Natalie had blinked at that. And had then hated herself, because the thing that wound around inside of her was not shame. It was far warmer and far more dangerous.

I never will again, she'd vowed. And she'd wanted to mean it with every fiber of her being. I swear.

You can do as you like with Rodolfo, Valentina had replied, and Natalie could almost hear the other woman's airy tone through the typed words. You have my blessing. Really. A hundred Eastern European models can't be wrong!

But it wasn't Valentina's blessing that she'd wanted, Natalie realized. Because that was a little too close to outright permission and she'd hardly been able to control herself as it was. What she wanted was outrage. Fury and consequences. Something— *anything*—to keep her from acting like a right tart.

And instead it was a little more than a week later and Rodolfo was outplaying her at the game she was very much afraid she'd put into motion that first day in her new role as the princess. By accident—or at least, without thinking about the consequences—but that hardly mattered now.

Worse, he was doing it masterfully, by not involving her at all. Why risk what might come out of her mouth when he could do an end run around her and go straight to King Geoffrey instead? On some level, Natalie admired the brilliance of the move. It made Rodolfo look like less of a libertine in the king's eyes and far more of the sort of political ally for Murin he would one day become as the King of Tissely.

She needed to stop underestimating her prince. Before she got into the kind of trouble a text couldn't solve.

"Prince Rodolfo thinks the two of you ought to build more of an accessible public profile ahead of the wedding," the king said as they'd sat at their third dinner of the week, as was apparently protocol.

It had taken Natalie a moment to realize Geoffrey was actually waiting for her response. She'd swallowed the bite of tender Murinese lamb she'd put in her mouth and smiled automatically, playing back what he'd said—because she'd gotten in the terrible habit of nodding along without really listening. She preferred to study the King's features and ask herself why, if he was her father, she didn't *feel* it. And he didn't either, clearly. Surely she should *know him* on a deep, cellular level. Or something. Wasn't blood supposed to reveal itself like that? And if it didn't, surely that meant that she and Valentina only happened to resemble each other by chance.

In every detail. Down to resembling Geoffrey, too. So much so that the King himself couldn't tell the difference when they switched.

Natalie knew on a level she didn't care to explore that it was unlikely to be chance. That it couldn't be chance.

"A public profile?" she echoed, because she had to say something, and she had an inkling that flatly refusing to do anything Rodolfo suggested simply because it had come from him wouldn't exactly fly as far as the king was concerned.

"I rather like the idea." King Geoffrey's attention had returned to his own plate. "It is a sad fact that in these modern times, a public figure is judged as much on the image he presents to the world as his contributions to it. More, perhaps."

He didn't order her to do as Rodolfo asked. But then, he didn't have to issue direct orders. And that was how Natalie found herself flying off to Rome to attend a star-studded charity gala the very next day, because Rodolfo had decided it was an excellent opportunity to "boost their profile" in the eyes of the international press corps.

If she ignored the reason she was taking the trip and the man who'd engineered it, Natalie had to admit that it was lovely to have her every need attended to, for a change. All she had to do was wake up the following morning. Everything else was sorted out by a fleet of others. Her wardrobe attendant asked if she had any particular requests and, when Natalie said she didn't, nodded decisively and returned with tidily packed luggage in less than an hour. Which footmen then whisked away. Natalie was swept off to the same private jet as before, where she was fed a lovely lunch of a complicated, savory salad and served sparkling water infused with cucumber. Things she didn't know she craved, deeply, until they were presented to her.

"Your chocolate, Your Highness," the air steward said with a smile after clearing away the salad dishes, presenting her with two rich, dark squares on a gold-embossed plate. "From the finest chocolatiers in all of the kingdom."

"I do like my chocolate," Natalie murmured.

More than that, she liked the princess's style, she thought as she let each rich, almost sweet square dissolve on her tongue, as if it had been crafted precisely to appeal to her.

Which, if she and Valentina were identical twins after all, she supposed it had.

And the pampering continued. The hotel she was delivered to in Rome, located at the top of the Spanish Steps to command the finest view possible over the ancient, vibrant city, had been arranged for and carefully screened by someone else. All she had to do was walk inside and smile as the staff all but kowtowed before her. Once in her sprawling penthouse suite, Natalie was required to do nothing but relax as her attendants bustled around, unpacking her things in one of the lavishly appointed rooms while they got to work on getting the princess ready for the gala in another. A job that required the undivided attention of a team of five stylists, apparently, when Natalie was used to tossing something on in the five minutes between crises and making the best of it.

Her fingernails were painted, her hair washed and cut and styled just so, and even her makeup was deftly applied. When they were done, Natalie was dressed like a fairy-tale princess all ready for her ball.

And her prince, something inside her murmured.

She shoved that away. Hard. There'd been no room for fairy tales in her life, only hard work and dedication. Her mother had told her stories that always ended badly, and Natalie had given up wishing for happier conclusions to such tales a long, long time ago. Even if she and Valentina really were sisters, it hardly mattered now. She was a grown woman. There was no being swept off in a pumpkin and spending the rest of her life surrounded by dancing mice. That ship had sailed.

She had no time for fairy tales. Not even if she happened to be living one.

Natalie concentrated on the fact that she looked like someone else tonight. Someone she recognized, yet didn't. Someone far more sophisticated than she'd ever been, and she'd thought her constant exposure to billionaires like Mr. Casilieris had given her a bit of polish.

You look like someone beautiful, she thought in a kind of wonder as she studied herself in the big, round mirror that graced the wall in her room. *Objectively beautiful.*

Her hair was swept up into a chignon and secured with pins that gleamed with quietly elegant jewels. Her dress was a dove-gray color that seemed to make her skin glow, cascading from a strapless bodice to a wide, gorgeous skirt that moved of its own accord when she walked and made her look very nearly celestial. Her shoes were high sandals festooned with straps, there was a clasp of impossible sapphires and diamonds at her throat that matched the ring she wore on her hand and her eyes looked fathomless.

Natalie looked like a princess. Not just Princess Valentina, but the sort of magical, fantasy princess she'd have told anyone who asked she'd never, ever imagined when she was a child, because she'd been taught better than that.

Never ever. Not once.

She nodded and smiled her thanks at her waiting attendants, but Natalie didn't dare speak. She was afraid that if she did, that faint catch in her throat would tip over into something far more embarrassing, and then worse, she'd have to explain it. And Natalie had no idea how to explain the emotions that buffeted her then.

Because the truth was, she didn't know how to be beautiful. She knew how to stick to the shadows and more, how to excel in them. She knew how to disappear in plain sight and use that to her—and her employer's—advantage. Natalie had no idea how to be the center of attention. How to be *seen*. In fact, she'd actively avoided it. Princess Valentina turned heads wherever she went, and Natalie had no idea how she was going to handle it. If she *could* handle it.

But it was more than her shocking appearance, so princessy and pretty. This was the first time in all her life that she hadn't had to be responsible for a thing. Not one thing. Not even her own sugar consumption, apparently. This was the first time in recent memory that she hadn't had to fix things for someone else or exhaust herself while making sure that others could relax and enjoy themselves.

No one had ever taken care of Natalie Monette. Not once. She'd had to become Princess Valentina for that to happen. And while she hadn't exactly expected that impersonating royalty would feel like a delightful vacation from her life, she hadn't anticipated that it would feel a bit more like an earthquake, shaking her apart from within.

It isn't real, a hard voice deep inside of her snapped, sounding a great deal like her chilly mother. *It's temporary and deeply stupid, as you should have known before you tried on that ring.*

Natalie knew that, of course. She flexed her hand at her side and watched the ring Prince Rodolfo had given another woman spill light here and there. None of this was real. Because none of this was hers. It was a short, confusing break from real life, that was all, and there was no use getting all soppy about it. There was only surviving it without blowing up the real princess's life while she was mucking around in it.

But all the bracing lectures in the world couldn't keep that glowing thing inside her chest from expanding as she gazed at the princess in the mirror, until it felt as if it was a part of every breath she took. Until she couldn't tell where the light of it ended and that shaking thing began. And she didn't need little voices inside of her to tell her how dangerous that was. She could feel it deep in her bones, knitting them into new shapes she was very much afraid she would have to break into pieces when she left.

Because whatever else this was, it was temporary. She needed to remember that above all.

"Your Highness." It was the most senior of the aides who traveled with the princess, something Natalie had known at a glance because she recognized the older woman's particular blend of sharp focus and efficient movement. "His Royal Highness Prince Rodolfo has arrived to escort you to the gala."

"Thank you," Natalie murmured, as serenely and princessy as possible.

And this was the trouble with dressing up like a beautiful princess who could be whisked off to a ball at a moment's notice. Natalie started to imagine that was exactly who she was. It was so hard to keep her head, and then she walked into the large, comfortably elegant living room of her hotel suite to find Prince Rodolfo waiting for her, decked out in evening clothes, and everything troubling became that much harder.

He stood at the great glass doors that slid open to one of the terraces that offered up stunning views of Rome at all times, but particularly now, as the sun inched toward the horizon and the city was bathed in a dancing, liquid gold.

More to the point, so was Rodolfo.

Natalie hadn't seen him since that unfortunate kissing incident. Not in person, anyway. And once again she was struck by the vast, unconquerable distance between pictures of the man on a computer screen and the reality before her. He stood tall and strong with his hands thrust into the pockets of trousers that had clearly been lovingly crafted to his precise, athletic measurements. His attention was on the red-and-gold sunset happening there before him, fanciful and lovely, taking over the Roman sky as if it was trying to court his favor.

He wasn't even looking at her. And still he somehow stole all the air from the room.

Natalie felt herself flush as she stood in the doorway, a long, deep roll of heat that scared her, it was so intense. Her pulse was a wild fluttering, everywhere. Her temples. Her throat. Her chest.

And deep between her legs, like an invitation she had no right to offer. Not this man. Not ever this man. If he was Prince Charming after all, and she was skeptical on that point, it didn't matter. He certainly wasn't hers.

She must have made some noise through that dry, clutching thing in her throat, because he turned to face her. And that wasn't any better. In her head, she'd downgraded the situation. She'd chalked it up to excusable nerves and understandable adrenaline over switching places with Valentina. That was the only explanation that had made any sense to her. She'd been so sure that when she saw Rodolfo again, all that power and compulsion that had sparked the air around him would be gone. He would just be another wealthy man for her to handle. Just another problem for her to solve.

But she'd been kidding herself.

If anything, tonight he was even worse, all dressed up in an Italian sunset.

Because you know, something inside her whispered. *You know, now.*

How he tasted. The feel of those lean, hard arms around her. The sensation of that marvelous mouth against hers. She had to fight back the shudder that she feared might bring her to her knees right there on the absurdly lush rug, but she had the sneaking suspicion he knew anyway. There was something about the curve of his mouth as he inclined his head.

"Princess," he murmured.

And God help her, but she felt that everywhere. *Everywhere.* As if he'd used his mouth directly against her heated skin.

"I hear you wish to build our public profile, whatever that is," she said, rather more severely than necessary. She made herself move forward, deeper into the room, when what she wanted to do was turn and run. She seated herself in an armchair because it meant he couldn't sit on either side of her, and his fascinating mouth twitched as if he knew exactly why she'd done it. "King Geoffrey—" She couldn't bring herself to say *my father,* not even if Valentina would have and not even if it was true "—was impressed. That is obviously the only reason I am here."

"Obviously." He threw himself onto the couch opposite her with the same reckless disregard for the lifespan of the average piece of furniture that he'd displayed back in Murin. She told herself that was reflective of his character. "Happily, it makes no difference to me if you are here of your own volition or not, so long as you are here."

"What a lovely sentiment. Every bride dreams of such poetry, I am certain. I am certainly aflutter."

"There is no need for sarcasm." But he sounded amused. "All that is required is that we appear in front of the paparazzi and look as if this wedding is our idea because we are a couple in love like any other, not simply a corporate merger with crowns."

Natalie eyed him, wishing the Roman sunset was not taking quite so long, nor quite so many liberties with Rodolfo's already impossible good looks. He was bathed in gold and russet now, and it made him glow, as if he was the sort of dream maidens might have had in this city thousands of years ago in feverish anticipation of their fierce gods descending from on high.

She tried to cast that fanciful nonsense out of her head, but it was impossible. Especially when he was making no particular effort to hide the hungry look in his dark gaze as he trained it on her. She could feel it shiver through her, lighting her on fire. Making it as hard to sit still as it was to breathe.

"I don't think anyone is going to believe that we were swept away by passion," she managed to say. She folded her hands in her lap the way she'd seen Valentina do in the videos she'd watched of the princess these past few nights, so worried was she that someone would be able to see right through her because she forgot to do some or other princessy thing. Though she thought she gripped her own fingers a bit more tightly than the princess had. "Seeing as how our engagement has been markedly free of any hint of it until now."

"But that's the beauty of it." Rodolfo shrugged. "The story could be that we were promised to each other and were prepared to do our duty, only to trip over the fact we were made for each other all along. Or it could be that it was never arranged at all and that we met, kept everything secret, and are now close enough to our wedding that we can let the world see what our hearts have always known."

"You sound like a tabloid."

"Thank you."

Natalie glared at him. "There is no possible way that could be construed as a compliment."

"I've starred in so many tabloid scandals I could write the headlines myself. And that is what we will do, starting tonight. We will rewrite whatever story is out there and make it into a grand romance. The Playboy Prince and His Perfect Princess, etcetera." That half smile of his deepened. "You get the idea, I'm sure."

"Why would we want to do something so silly? You are going to be a king, not a Hollywood star. Surely a restrained, distant competence is more the package you should be presenting to the world." Natalie aimed her coolest smile at him. "Though I grant you, that might well be another difficult reach."

The sun finally dripped below the city as she spoke, leaving strands of soft pink and deep gold in its wake. But it also made it a lot easier to see Prince Rodolfo's dark, measuring expression. And much too easy to feel the way it clattered through her, making her feel...jittery.

It occurred to her that the way he lounged there, so carelessly, was an optical illusion. Because there wasn't a single thing about him that wasn't hard and taut, as if he not only kept all his brooding power on a tight leash—but could explode into action at any moment. That notion was not exactly soothing.

Neither was his smile. "We will spend the rest of the night in public, princess. Fawned over by the masses. So perhaps you will do me the favor of telling me here, in private, exactly what it is that has made you imagine I deserve a steady stream of insult. One after the next, without end, since I last saw you."

Natalie felt chastened by that, and hated herself for it in the next instant. Because her own feelings didn't matter here. She shouldn't even have feelings where this man was concerned. Valentina might have given her blessing to whatever happened between her betrothed and Natalie, but that was neither here nor there. Natalie knew better than to let a man like this beguile her. She'd been taught to see through this sort of thing at her mother's knee. It appalled her that his brand of patented princely charm was actually *working*.

"Are you not deserving?" she asked quietly. She made herself meet his dark gaze, though something inside her quailed at it. And possibly died a little bit, too. But she didn't look away. "Are you sure?"

"Am I a vicious man?" Rodolfo's voice was no louder than hers, but there was an intensity to it that made that lick of shame inside of her shimmer, then expand. It made the air in the room seem thin. It made Natalie's heart hit at her ribs, hard enough to bruise. "A brute? A monster in some fashion?"

"Only you can answer that question, I think."

"I am unaware of any instance in which I have deliberately hurt another person, but perhaps you, princess, know something I do not about my own life."

It turned out the Prince was as effective with a

slap down as her boss. Natalie sat a bit straighter, but she didn't back down. "Everyone knows a little too much about your life, Your Highness. Entirely too much, one might argue."

"Tabloid fantasies are not life. They are a game. You should know that better than anyone, as we sit here discussing a new story we plan to sell ourselves."

"How would I know this, exactly?" She felt her head tilt to one side in a manner she thought was more her than Valentina. She corrected it. "I do not appear in the tabloids. Not with any frequency, and only on the society pages. Never the front-page stories." Natalie knew. She'd checked.

"You are a paragon, indeed." Rodolfo's voice was low and dark and not remotely complimentary. "But a rather judgmental one, I fear."

Natalie clasped her hands tighter together. "That word has always bothered me. There is nothing wrong with rendering judgment. It's even lauded in some circles. How did *judgmental* become an insult?"

"When rendering judgment became a blood sport," Rodolfo replied, with a soft menace that drew blood on its own.

But Natalie couldn't stop to catalog the wounds it left behind, all over her body, or she was afraid she'd simply…collapse.

"It is neither bloody nor sporting to commit yourself to a woman in the eyes of the world and then continue to date others, Your Highness," she said crisply. "It is simply unsavory. Perhaps childish. And certainly dishonorable. I think you'll find that there are very few women on the planet who will judge that behavior favorably."

Rodolfo inclined his head, though she had the sense his jaw was tighter than it had been. "Fair enough. I will say in my defense that you never seemed to care one way or the other what I did, much less with whom, before last week. We talked about it at length and you said nothing. Not one word."

Valentina had said he talked at her, defending himself—hadn't she? Natalie couldn't remember. But she also wasn't here to poke holes in Valentina's story. It didn't matter if it was true. It mattered that she'd felt it, and Natalie could do something to help fix it. Or try, anyway.

"You're right, of course," she said softly, keeping her gaze trained to his. "It's my fault for not fore-seeing that your word was not your bond and your vows were meaningless. My deepest apologies. I'll be certain to keep all of that in mind on our wedding day."

He didn't appear to move, and yet suddenly Natalie couldn't, as surely as if he'd reached out and wrapped her in his tight grip. His dark gaze seemed to pin her to her chair, intent and hard.

"I've tasted you," he reminded her, as if she could forget that for an instant. As if she hadn't dreamed about exactly that, night after night, waking up with his taste on her tongue and a deep, restless ache between her legs. "I know you want me, yet you fight me. Is it necessary to you that I become the villain? Does that make it easier?"

Natalie couldn't breathe. Her heart felt as if it might rip its way out of her chest all on its own, and she still couldn't tear her gaze away from his. There was that hunger, yes, but also a kind of *certainty* that made her feel...liquid.

"Because it is not necessary to insult me to get my attention, princess," Rodolfo continued in the same intense way. "You have it. And you need not question my fidelity. I will touch no other but you, if that is what you require. Does this satisfy you? Can we step away from the bloodlust, do you think?"

What that almost offhanded promise did was make Natalie feel as if she was nothing but a puppet and he was pulling all her strings, all without laying a single finger upon her. And what sent an arrow of shame and delight spiraling through her was that she couldn't tell if she was properly horrified by that notion, or...not.

"Don't be ridiculous," was the best she could manage.

"You only confirm my suspicions," he told her then, and she knew she wasn't imagining the satisfaction that laced his dark tone. "It is not who I might or might not have dated over the past few months that so disturbs you. I do not doubt that is a factor, but it is not the whole picture. Will you tell me what is? Or will I be forced to guess?"

And she knew, somehow, that his guesses would involve his hands on her once more and God help her, she didn't know what might happen if he touched her again. She didn't know what she might do. Or not do.

Who she might betray, or how badly.

She stood then, moving to put the chair between them, aware of the way her magnificent gown swayed and danced as if it had a mind of its own. And of the way Rodolfo watched her do it, that hard-lit amusement in his dark eyes, as if she were acting precisely as he'd expected she would.

As if he was a rather oversize cat toying with his next meal and was in absolutely no doubt as to how this would all end.

Though she didn't really care to imagine him treating her like his dinner. Or, more precisely, she refused to allow herself to imagine it, no matter how her pulse rocketed through her veins.

"My life is about order," she said, and she realized as she spoke that she wasn't playing her prescribed role. That the words were pouring out of a part of her she hadn't even known was there inside of her. "I have duties, responsibilities, and I handle them all. I *like* to handle them. I like knowing that I'm equal to any task that's put in front of me, and then proving it. Especially when no one thinks I can."

"And you are duly celebrated for your sense of duty throughout the great houses of Europe." Rodolfo inclined his head. "I salute you."

"I can't tell if you're mocking me or not, but I don't require celebration," she threw back at him. "It's not about that. It's about the accomplishment. It's about putting an order to things no matter how messy they get."

"Valentina..."

Natalie was glad he said that name. It reminded her who she was—and who she wasn't. It allowed her to focus through all the clamor and spin inside of her.

"But your life is chaos," she said, low and fierce. "As far as I can tell, it always has been. I think you must like it that way, as you have been careening from one death wish to another since your brother—"

"Careful."

He looked different then, furious and something like thrown, but she only lifted her chin and told herself to ignore it. Because the pain of an international playboy had nothing to do with her. Prince Charming was the villain in all the stories her mother had told her, never the hero. And the brother he'd lost when he was fifteen was a means to psychoanalyze this man, not humanize him. She told herself that again and again. And then she forged on.

"He died, Rodolfo. You lived." He hissed in a breath as if she'd struck him, but Natalie didn't stop. "And yet your entire adult life appears to be a calculated attempt to change that. You and I have absolutely nothing in common."

Rodolfo stood. The glittering emotion she'd seen grip him a moment ago was in his dark gaze, ferocious and focused, but he was otherwise wiped clean. She would have been impressed if she'd been able to breathe.

"My brother's death was an unfortunate tragedy." But he sounded something like hollow. As if he was reciting a speech he'd learned by rote a long time ago. His gaze remained irate and focused on her. "I never intended to fill his shoes and, in fact, make no attempt to do so. I like extreme sports, that is all. It isn't a death wish. I am neither suicidal nor reckless."

He might as well have been issuing his own press release.

"If you die while leaping out of helicopters to get to the freshest ski slope in the world, the way you famously do week after week in winter, you will not only break your neck and likely die, you will leave your country in chaos," Natalie said quietly. His gaze intensified, but she didn't look away. "It all comes back to chaos, Your Highness. And that's not me."

She expected him to rage at her. To argue. She expected that dark thing in him to take him over, and she braced herself for it. If she was honest, she was waiting for him to reach out and his put his hands on her again the way he had the last time. She was waiting for his kiss as surely as if he'd cast a spell and that was her only hope of breaking it—

It was astonishing, really, how much of a fool she was when it counted.

But Rodolfo's hard, beguiling mouth only curved

as if there wasn't a world of seething darkness in his eyes, and somehow that sent heat spiraling all the way through her.

"Maybe it should be, princess," he said softly, so softly, as if he was seducing her where he stood. As if he was the spell and there was no breaking it, not when he was looking at her like that, as if no one else existed in all the world. "Maybe a little chaos is exactly what you need."

CHAPTER SIX

THE CHARITY GALA took place in a refurbished ancient villa, blazing with light and understated wealth and dripping with all manner of international celebrities like another layer of decoration. Icons from the epic films of Bollywood mingled with lauded stars of the stages of the West End and rubbed shoulders with a wide selection of Europe's magnificently blooded aristocrats, all doing what they did best. They graced the red carpet as if they found nothing more delightful, smiling into cameras and posing for photographs while giving lip service to the serious charity cause du jour.

Rodolfo escorted his mouthy, surprising princess down the gauntlet of the baying paparazzi, smiling broadly as the press went mad at the sight of them, just as he'd suspected they would.

"I told you," he murmured, leaning down to put his mouth near her ear. As much to sell the story of their great romance as to take pleasure in the way she shivered, then stiffened as if she was trying to hide it from him. Who could have imagined that his distant betrothed was so exquisitely sensitive? He couldn't wait to find out where else she was this tender. This sweet. "They want nothing more than to imagine us wildly and madly in love."

"A pity my imagination is not quite so vivid," she replied testily, though she did it through a smile that perhaps only he could tell was not entirely serene.

But the grin on Rodolfo's face as they made their way slowly through the wall of flashing cameras and shouting reporters wasn't feigned in the least.

"You didn't mention which charity this gala benefits," the princess said crisply as they followed the well-heeled crowd inside the villa, past dramatic tapestries billowing in the slight breeze and a grand pageant of colored lights in the many fountains along the way.

"Something critically important, I am sure," he replied, and his grin only deepened when she slid a reproving look at him. "Surely they are all important, princess. In the long run, does it matter which one this is?"

"Not to you, clearly," she murmured, nodding regally at yet another photographer. "I am sure your carelessness—excuse me, I mean thoughtfulness—is much appreciated by all the charities around who benefit from your random approach."

Rodolfo resolved to take her out in public every night, to every charity event he could find in Europe, whether he'd heard of its cause or not. Not only because she was stunning and he liked looking at her, though that helped. The blazing lights caught the red in her hair and made it shimmer. The gray dress she wore hugged her figure before falling in soft waves to the floor. She was a vision, and better than all of that, out here in the glare of too many spotlights she could not keep chairs between them to ward him off. He liked the heat of her arm through his. He liked her body beside his, lithe and slender as if she'd been crafted to fit him. He liked the faint scent of her, a touch of something French and something sweet besides, and below it, the simplicity of that soap she used.

There wasn't much he didn't like about this woman, if he was honest, not even her intriguing puritan streak. Or her habit of poking at him the way no one else had ever dared, not even his disapproving father, who preferred to express his endless disappointment with far less sharpness and mockery. No one else ever threw Felipe in his face and if they'd ever tried to do such a remarkably stupid thing, it certainly wouldn't have been to psychoanalyze him. Much less find him wanting.

He took care of that all on his own, no doubt. And the fact that his own father found his second son so much more lacking than his first was common knowledge and obvious to all. No need to underscore it.

Rodolfo supposed it was telling that as little as he cared to have that conversation, he hadn't minded that Valentina had tried. Or he didn't mind too much.

He didn't know where his deferential, disappearing princess had gone, the one who had hidden in plain sight when there'd been no one in the room but the two of them, but he liked this one much better.

The hardest part of his body agreed. Enthusiastically. And it didn't much care that they were out in public.

But there was another gauntlet to run inside the villa. One Rodolfo should perhaps have anticipated.

"I take it that you did not make proclamations about your sudden onset of fidelity to your many admirers," Valentina said dryly after they were stopped for the fifth time in as many steps by yet another woman who barely glanced at the princess and then all but melted all over Rodolfo. Right there in front of her.

For the first time in his entire adult life, Rodolfo found he was faintly embarrassed by his own prowess with the fairer sex.

"It is not the sort of thing one typically announces," he pointed out, while attempting to cling to his dignity, despite the number of slinky women circling him with that same avid look in their eyes. "It has the whiff of desperation about it, does it not?

"Of course, generally speaking, becoming engaged *is* the announcement." What was wrong with him, that he found her tartness so appealing? Especially when not a bit of it showed on her lovely, serene face? How had he spent all these months failing to notice how appealing she was? He'd puzzled it over for days and still couldn't understand it. "I can see the confusion in your case, given your exploits these last months."

"Yet here I am," he pointed out, slanting a look down at her, amused despite himself. "At your side. Exuding fidelity."

"That is not precisely what you exude," she said under her breath, because naturally she couldn't let any opportunity pass to dig at him, and then they were swept into the receiving line.

It felt like a great many hours later when they finally made it into the actual gala itself. A band played on a raised dais while glittering people outshone the blazing chandeliers above them. Europe's finest and fanciest stood in these rooms, and he'd estimate that almost all of them had their eyes fixed on the spectacle of Prince Rodolfo and Princess Valentina actually out and about together for once—without a single one of their royal relatives in sight as the obvious puppeteers of what had been hailed everywhere as an entirely cold-blooded marriage of royal convenience.

But their presence here had already done exactly what Rodolfo had hoped it would. He could see it in the faces of the people around them. He'd felt it on the red carpet outside, surrounded by paparazzi nearly incandescent with joy over the pictures they'd be able to sell of the two of them. He could already read the accompanying headlines.

Do the Daredevil Prince and the Dutiful Princess Actually Like *Each Other After All?*

He could feel the entire grand ballroom of the villa seem to swell with the force of all that speculation and avid interest.

And Rodolfo made a command decision. They could do another round of the social niceties that would cement the story he wanted to sell even further, assuming he wasn't deluged by more of the sort of women who were happy to ignore his fiancée as she stood beside him. Or he could do what he really wanted to do, which was get his hands on Valentina right here in public, where she would have no choice but to allow it.

This was what he was reduced to. On some level, he felt the requisite shame. Or some small shadow of it, if he was honest.

Because it still wasn't much of a contest.

"Let's dance, shall we?" he asked, but he was already moving toward the dance floor in the vast, sparkling ballroom that seemed to swirl around him as he spoke. His proper, perfect princess would have to yank her arm out of his grip with some force, creating a scene, if she wanted to stop him.

He was sure he could see steam come off her as she realized that for herself, then didn't do it. Mutinously, if that defiant angle of her pointed chin was any clue.

"I don't dance," she informed him coolly as he stopped and turned to face her. He dropped her arm but stood a little too close to her, so the swishing skirt of her long dress brushed against his legs. It made her have to tip her head back to meet his gaze. And he was well aware it created the look of an intimacy between them. It suggested all kinds of closeness, just as he wanted it to do.

As much to tantalize the crowd as to tempt her.

"Are you certain?" he asked idly.

"Of course I'm certain."

Other guests waltzed around them, pretending not to stare as they stood still in the center of the dance floor as if they were having an intense discussion. Possibly an argument. Inviting gossip and rumor with every moment they failed to move. But Rodolfo forgot about all the eyes trained on them in the next breath. He gazed down at his princess, watching as the strangest expression moved over her face. Had she been anyone else, he would have called it panic.

"Then I fear I must remind you that you have been dancing since almost before you could walk," he replied, trying to keep his voice mild and a little bit lazy, as if that could hide the intensity of his need to touch her. As if every moment he did not was killing him. He felt as if it was.

He reached over and took her hands in his, almost losing his cool when he felt that simple touch everywhere—from his fingers to his feet and deep in his aching sex—far more potent than whole weekends he could hardly recall with women he wouldn't remember if they walked up and introduced themselves right now. What the hell was she doing to him? But he ordered himself to pull it together.

"There is that iconic portrait of you dancing with your father at some or other royal affair. It was the darling of the fawning press for years. You are standing on his shoes while the King of Murin dances for the both of you." Rodolfo made himself smile, as if the odd intensity that gripped him was nothing but a passing thing. The work of a moment, here and then gone in the swirl of the stately dance all around them. "I believe you were six."

"Six," she repeated. He thought she said it oddly, but then she seemed to recollect herself. He saw her blink, then focus on him again. "You misunderstand me. I meant that I don't dance with *you*. By which I mean, I won't."

"It pains me to tell you that, sadly, you are wrong yet again." He smiled at her, then indulged himself— and infuriated her—by reaching out to tug on one of the artful pieces of hair that had been left free of the complicated chignon she wore tonight. He tucked it behind her ear, marveling that so small a touch should echo inside of him the way it did then, sensation chasing sensation, as if all these months of not quite seeing her in front of him had been an exercise in restraint instead of an oddity he couldn't explain to his satisfaction. And this was his reward. "You will dance with me at our wedding, in front of the entire world. And no doubt at a great many affairs of state thereafter. It is unavoidable, I am afraid."

She started to frown, then caught herself. He saw the way she fought it back, and he still couldn't understand why it delighted him on a deep, visceral level. His glass princess, turned flesh and blood and brought to life right there before him. He could see the way her lips trembled, very slightly, and he knew somehow that it was the same mad fire that blazed in him, brighter by the moment.

It made him want nothing more than to taste her here and now, the crowd and royal protocol be damned.

"You should know that I make it a policy to step on the feet of all the men I dance with, as homage to that iconic photograph." Her smile was razor sharp and her eyes had gone cool again, but he could still see that soft little tremor that made her mouth too soft. Too vulnerable. He could still see the truth she clearly wanted to hide, and no matter that he couldn't name it. "Prepare yourself."

"All you need to do is follow my lead, princess," Rodolfo said then, low and perhaps a bit too dark, and he didn't entirely mean the words to take on an added resonance as he said them. But he smiled when she pulled in a sharp little breath, as if she was imagining all the places he could lead her, just as he was. In vivid detail. "It will be easy and natural. There will be no trodding upon feet. Simply surrender—" and his voice dipped a bit at that, getting rough in direct correlation to that dark, needy thing in her gaze "—and I will take care of you. I promise."

Rodolfo wasn't talking about dancing—or he wasn't only talking about a very public waltz—but that would do. He studied Princess Valentina as she stood there before him, taut and very nearly quivering with the same dark need that made him want to behave like a caveman instead of a prince. He wanted to throw her over his shoulder and carry her off into the night. He wanted to throw her down on the floor where they stood and get his mouth on every part of her, as if he could taste what it was that had changed in her, cracking her open to let the fascinating creature inside come out and making her irresistible seemingly overnight.

He settled for extending his hand, very formally and in full view of half of Europe, even throwing in a polite bow that, as someone more or less equal in rank to her, could only be construed as a magnanimous, even romantic gesture. Then he stood still in the center of the dance floor and waited for her to take it.

Her green eyes looked a little bit too wide and still far too dark with all the same simmering need and deep hunger he knew burned bright in him. She looked more beautiful than he'd ever seen her before, but then, he was closer than he'd ever been. He couldn't count those hot, desperate moments in the palace reception room where he'd tasted her with all the finesse of an untried adolescent, because he'd been too out of control—and out of his mind—to enjoy it.

This was different. This—tonight—he had every intention of savoring.

But he wasn't sure he would ever savor anything more than when she lifted that chin of hers, faintly pointed and filled with a defiance her vulnerable mouth contradicted, and placed her hand in his.

Rodolfo felt that everywhere, as potent as if she'd knelt down before him and declared him victor of this dark and delicious little war of theirs.

He pulled her a step closer with his right hand, then slid his left around to firmly clasp the back she'd left bared in the lovely dress she wore that poured over her slender figure like rain, and he heard her hiss in a breath. He could feel the heat of her like a furnace beneath his palm. He wanted to bend close and get his mouth on her more than he could remember wanting anything.

But he refrained. Somehow, he held himself in check, when he was a man who usually did the exact opposite. For fun.

"Put your hand on my shoulder," he told her, and he didn't sound urbane or witty or anything like lazy. Not anymore. "Have you truly forgotten how to perform a simple waltz, princess? I am delighted to discover how deeply I affect you."

He felt the hard breath she took, as if she was bracing herself. And he realized with a little shock that he had no idea what she would do. It was as likely that she'd yank herself out of his arms and storm away as it was that she'd melt into him. He had no idea—and he couldn't deny he felt that like a long, slow lick against the hardest part of him.

She was as unpredictable as one of his many adventures. He had the odd thought that he could spend a lifetime trying to unravel her mysteries, one after the next, and who knew if he'd ever manage it? It astonished him that he wanted to try. That for the first time since their engagement last fall, he wanted their wedding day to hurry up and arrive. And better than that, their wedding night. And all the nights thereafter, all those adventures lined up and waiting for him, packed into her lush form and those fathomless green eyes.

He could hardly wait.

And it felt as if ten years had passed when, with her wary gaze trained on him as if he couldn't be trusted not to harm her somehow, Valentina put her hand where it belonged.

"Thank you, princess." He curled his fingers around hers a little tighter than necessary for the sheer pleasure of it and smiled when the hand she'd finally placed on his shoulder dug into him, as if in reaction. "You made that into quite a little bit of theater. When stories emerge tomorrow about the great row we had in the middle of a dance floor, you will have no one to blame but yourself."

"I never do," she replied coolly, but that wariness receded from her green gaze. Her chin tipped up higher and Rodolfo counted it as a win. "It's called taking responsibility for myself, which is another way of acknowledging that I'm an adult. You should try it sometime."

"Impossible," he said, gripping her hand tighter in his and smiling for all those watching eyes. And because her defiance made him want to smile, which was far more dangerous. And exciting. "I am far too busy leaping out of planes in a vain attempt to cheat death. Or court death. Which is it again? I can't recall which accusation you leveled at me, much less when."

And before she could enlighten him, he started to move.

She was stiff in his arms, which he assumed was another form of protest. Rodolfo ignored it, sweeping her around the room and leading her through the steps she appeared to be pretending not to know, just as he'd promised he would.

"You cannot trip me up, princess," he told her when she relaxed just slightly in his hold and gave herself over to his lead. "I was raised to believe a man can only call himself a man when he knows how to dance well, shoot with unerring accuracy and argue his position without either raising his voice or reducing himself to wild, unjustified attacks on his opponent."

"Well," she said, and she sounded breathless, which he felt in every part of his body like an ache, "you obviously took that last part to heart."

"I am also an excellent shot, thank you for asking."

"Funny, the tabloids failed to report that. Unless you're speaking in innuendo? In which case, I must apologize, but I don't speak twelve-year-old boy."

He let out a laugh that had the heads nearest them turning, because no one was ever so giddy when on display like this, especially not him. Rodolfo was infamous because he called attention to himself in other ways, but never like this. Never in situations like these, all stuffy protocol and too many spectators. Never with anything that might be confused for *joy*.

"You must be feeling better if you're this snappish, princess."

"I wasn't feeling bad. Unless you count the usual dismay anyone might feel at being bullied onto a dance floor in the company of a rather alarming man who dances very much like he flings himself off the sides of mountains."

"With a fierce and provocative elegance? The envy of all who witness it?"

"With astonishing recklessness and a total lack of regard for anyone around you. Much in the same vein as your entire life, Your Highness, if the reports are true." She lifted one shoulder, then let it drop in as sophisticated and dismissive a shrug as he'd ever seen. "Or even just a little bit true, for that matter."

"And if you imagine that was bullying, princess, you have led a very charmed life, indeed. Even for a member of a royal house dating back to, oh, the start of recorded history or thereabouts, surrounded by wealth and ease at every turn."

"What do you want, Rodolfo?" she asked then, and that near-playful note he was sure he'd heard in her voice was gone. Her expression was grave. As if she was yet another stranger, this one different than before. "I don't believe that this marriage is anything you would have chosen, if given the opportunity. I can't imagine why you're suddenly pretending otherwise and proclaiming your commitment to fidelity in random hotel suites. What I do understand is that we're both prepared to do our duty and have been from the start. And I support that, but there's nothing wrong with maintaining a civil, respectful distance while we go about it."

"I would have agreed with you in every respect," he said, and he should have been worried about that fervent intensity in his tone. He could feel the flames of it licking through him, changing him, making him something other than the man he'd thought he was all this time. Something that should have set off alarms in every part of him, yet didn't. "But that was before you walked into your father's reception rooms and rather than blending into the furniture the way you usually did, opted to attack me instead."

"Of course." And Rodolfo had the strangest sensation that she was studying him as if he was a museum exhibit, not her fiancé. Hardly even a man—which should have chastened him. Instead, it made him harder. "I should have realized that to a man like you, with an outsize ego far more vast and unconquerable than any of the mountain peaks you've summited in your desperate quest for meaning, any questioning of any kind is perceived as an attack."

"You are missing the point, I think," Rodolfo said, making no attempt to hide either the laughter in his voice or the hunger in his gaze, not put off by her character assassinations at all. Quite the opposite. "Attack me all you like. It doesn't shame me in the least. Surely you must be aware that *shame* is not the primary response I have to you, princess. It is not even close."

She didn't ask him what he felt instead, but he saw a betraying, bright flush move over her face. And he knew she was perfectly aware of the things that moved in him, sensation and need, hunger and that edgy passion—and more, that she felt it, too.

Perhaps that was why, when they danced past a set of huge, floor-to-ceiling glass doors that led out to a wide terrace for the third time, he led her out into the night instead of deeper into the ballroom.

"Where are we going?" she asked.

Rodolfo thought it was meant to be a demand—a rebuke, even—but her cheeks were too red. Her eyes were too bright. And most telling, she made no attempt to tug her hand from his, much less lecture him any further about chaos and order and who was on which side of that divide.

"Nothing could be less chaotic than a walk on a terrace in full view of so many people," he pointed out, not bothering to look behind him at the party they'd left in full swing. He had no doubt they were all staring after him, the way they always did, and with more intensity than ever because he was with Valentina. "Unless you'd like it to be?"

"Certainly not. Some people admire the mountain from afar, Your Highness. They are perfectly happy doing so, and feel no need whatsoever to throw themselves off it or climb up it or attempt to ski down the back of it."

"Ah, but some people do not live, princess. They merely exist."

"Risking death is not living. It's nihilistic. And in your case, abominably selfish."

"Perhaps." He held her hand tighter in his. "But I would not underestimate the power of a little bout of selfishness, if I were you. Indulge yourself, princess. Just for an evening. What's the worst that could happen?"

"I shudder to think," she retorted, but there was no heat in it.

Rodolfo pretended not to hear the catch in her throat. But he smiled. He liberated two glasses of something exquisite from a passing servant with a tray, he pulled his fascinating princess closer to his side and then he led her deeper into the dark.

CHAPTER SEVEN

MAYBE IT WAS the music. Maybe it was the whirl of so many gleaming, glorious people.

Natalie had the suspicion that really, it was Ro-dolfo.

But no matter what it was, no matter why—she forgot.

That she wasn't really a princess, or if she was, she was the discarded kind. The lost and never-meant-to-be-found sort that had only been located by accident in a bathroom outside London.

She forgot that the dress wasn't hers, the ball inside the pretty old building wasn't a magical spectacle put on just for her and, most of all, that the man at her side—gripping her hand as he led her into temptation—wasn't ever going to be hers, no matter what.

He'd danced with her. It was as simple and as complicated as that.

Natalie had never thought of herself as beautiful before she'd seen herself in that mirror tonight, but it was more than that. She couldn't remember the last time anyone had treated her like a *woman*. Much less a desirable one. Not a pawn in whatever game the man in question might have been playing with her employer, which had only ever led to her wearing her hair in severe ponytails and then donning those clear glasses to keep the attention off her. Not an assistant. Not the person responsible for every little detail of every little thing and therefore the first one to be upbraided when something went wrong.

Rodolfo looked at her as if she was no more and no less than a beautiful woman. He didn't see a list of all the things she could *do* when he gazed at her. He saw only her. A princessed-out, formally made-up version of her, sure. And she couldn't really gloss over the fact he called her by the wrong name because he had every reason to believe she was someone else. Even so, she was the woman he couldn't seem to stop touching, who made his eyes light up with all that too-bright need and hunger.

And it was that, Natalie found, she couldn't resist.

She'd never done a spontaneous thing in her life before she'd switched places with Valentina in that bathroom. Left to her own devices, she thought it was likely she'd never have given her notice at all, no matter how worked up she'd been. And now it seemed she couldn't stop with the spontaneity. Yet somehow Rodolfo's grip on her hand, so strong and sure, made her not mind very much at all. She let this prince, who was far more charming than she wanted to admit to herself, tug her along with him, deeper into the shadows, until they were more in the dark than the light.

He turned to face her then, and he looked something like stern in the darkness. He set the two glasses of sparkling wine down on the nearby balustrade, then straightened again. Slowly. Deliberately, even. Natalie's heart thudded hard against her ribs, but it wasn't from fear. He pulled her hand that he'd been holding high against his chest and held it there, and Natalie couldn't have said why she felt as caught. As gripped tight. Only that she was—and more concerning, had no desire to try to escape it.

If anything, she leaned closer into him, into the shelter of his big body.

"Where did you come from?" he asked, his voice a mere scrape against the night. "What the hell are you doing to me?"

Natalie opened her mouth to answer him. But whatever that dark, driving force had been inside her, urging her to poke back at him and do her best to slap down the only real Prince Charming she'd ever met in the flesh, it was gone. Had she imagined herself some kind of avenging angel here? Flying into another woman's royal fairy tale of a life to do what needed doing, the way she did with everything else? Fighting her mother's battles all these years later and with a completely different man than the one Erica had never explicitly named?

It didn't matter, because that had been before he'd taken her in his arms and guided her around a dance floor, making her feel as if she could dance forever when she'd never danced a waltz before in her life. She had a vague idea of what it entailed, but only because she'd had to locate the best ballroom dancing instructor in London when Achilles Casilieris had abruptly decided he needed a little more polish one year. She'd watched enough of those classes— before Mr. Casilieris had reduced the poor man to tears—to understand the basic principle of a waltz.

But Rodolfo had made her feel as if they were flying.

He looked down at her now, out here in the seductive dark, and it made her tremble deep inside. It made her forget who she was and what she was doing. Her head cleared of everything save him. Rodolfo. The daredevil prince who made her feel as if she was the one catapulting herself out of airplanes every time his dark, hungry gaze caught hers. And held.

He took her bare shoulders in his hands, drawing her closer to him. Making her shiver, deep and long. On some distant level she thought she should push away from him. Remind them both of her boundaries, maybe. But she couldn't seem to remember what those were. Instead she tilted her head back while she drifted closer to his big, rangy body. And then she made everything worse by sliding her hands over the steel wall of his chest, carefully packaged in that gorgeous suit that made him look almost edible. To push him away, she told herself piously.

But she didn't push at him. She didn't even try.

His dark eyes gleamed with a gold she could feel low in her belly, like a fiery caress. "The way you look at me is dangerous, princess."

"I thought you courted danger," she heard herself whisper.

"I do," he murmured. "Believe me, I do."

And then he bent his head and kissed her.

This time, the first brush of his mouth against hers was light. Easy. Electricity sparked and sizzled, and then he did it again, and it wasn't enough. Natalie pressed herself toward him, trying to get more of him. Trying to crawl inside him and throw herself into the storm that roared through her. She went up on her toes to close the remaining distance between them, and her reward was the way he smiled, that dangerous curve of his mouth against hers.

It seemed to wash over her like heat then pool in a blaze of fire, high between her legs. Natalie couldn't keep herself from letting out a moan, needy and insistent.

And obvious. So terribly, blatantly obvious it might as well have been a scream in the dark. She felt Rodolfo turn to stone beneath her palms.

Then he angled his head, took the kiss deeper and wilder and everything went mad.

Rodolfo simply...took her over. He kissed her like he was already a great king and she but one more subject to his rule. His inimitable will. He kissed her as if there had never been any doubt that she was his, in every possible way. His mouth was demanding and hot, intense and carnal, and her whole body thrilled to it. Her hands were fists, gripping his jacket as if she couldn't bear to let go of him, and he only took the kiss deeper, wilder.

She arched against him as he plundered her mouth, taking and taking and taking even more as he bent her over his arm, as if he could never get enough—

Then he stopped, abruptly, muttering a curse against her lips. It seemed to pain him to release her, but he did it, stepping back and maneuvering so he stood between Natalie and what it took her far too long to realize was another group of guests making use of the wide terrace some distance away.

But she couldn't bring herself to care about them. She raised a hand to her lips, aware that her fingers trembled. And far more aware that he was watching her too closely as she did it.

"Why do you look at me as if it is two hundred years ago and I have just stolen your virtue?" he asked softly, his dark eyes searching hers. "Or led you to your ruin with a mere kiss?"

Natalie didn't know what look she wore on her face, but she felt…altered. There was no pretending otherwise. Rodolfo was looking at her the way any man might gaze at the woman he was marrying in less than two months, after kissing her very nearly senseless on the terrace of a romantic Roman villa.

But that was the trouble. No matter what fairy tale

she'd been spinning out in her head, Natalie wasn't that woman.

She was ruined, all right. All the way through.

"I'm not looking at you like that." Her voice hardly sounded like hers. She took a step away from him, coming up against the stone railing. She glanced down at the two glasses of sparkling wine that sat there and considered tossing them back, one after the next, because that might dull the sharp thing that felt a little too much like pain, poking inside of her. Only the fact that it might dull her a little *too* much kept her from it. Things were already bad enough. "I'm not looking at you like anything, I'm sure."

Rodolfo watched her, his eyes too dark to read. "You are looking at me as if you have never been kissed before. Much as that might pander to my ego, which I believe we've agreed is egregiously large already, we both know that isn't true." His mouth curved. "And tell the truth, Valentina. It was not so bad, was it?"

That name slammed into her like a sucker punch. Natalie could hardly breathe through it. She had to grit her teeth to keep from falling over where she stood. How did she keep forgetting?

Because you want to forget, a caustic voice inside her supplied at once.

"I'm not who you think I am," she blurted out then, and surely she wasn't the only one who could hear how ragged she sounded. How distraught.

But Rodolfo only laughed. "You are exactly who I think you are."

"I assure you, I am not. At all."

"It is an odd moment for a philosophical turn, princess," he drawled, and there was something harder about him then. Something more dangerous. Natalie could feel it dance over her skin. "Are any of us who others think we are? Take me, for example. I am certain that every single person at this gala tonight would line up to tell you exactly who I am, and they would be wrong. I am not the tabloid stories they craft about me, pimped out to the highest bidder. My wildest dream is not surviving an adventure or planning a new one, it's taking my rightful place in my father's kingdom. That's all." His admission, stark and raw, hung between them like smoke. She had the strangest notion that he hadn't meant to say anything like that. But in the next instant he looked fierce. Almost forbidding. "We are none of us the roles we play, I am sure."

"Are you claiming you have a secret inner life devoted to your sense of duty? That you are merely misunderstood?" she asked, incredulous.

"Do you take everything at face value, princess?" She told herself she was imagining that almost hurt look on his face. And it was gone when he angled his head toward her. "You cannot really believe you are the only one with an internal life."

"That's not what I meant."

But, of course, she couldn't tell him what she

meant. She couldn't explain that she hadn't been feeling the least bit philosophical. Or that she wasn't actually Princess Valentina at all. She certainly couldn't tell this man that she was Natalie Monette— a completely different person.

Though it occurred to her for the first time that even if she came clean right here and now, the likelihood was that he wouldn't believe her. Because who could believe something so fantastical? Would she have believed it herself if it wasn't happening to her right now—if she wasn't standing in the middle of another woman's life?

And messing it up beyond recognition, that same interior voice sniped at her. *Believe that, if nothing else.*

"Do you plan to tell me what, then, you meant?" Rodolfo asked, dark and low and maybe with a hint of asperity. Maybe with more than just a hint. "Or would you prefer it if I guessed?"

The truth hit Natalie then, with enough force that she felt it shake all the way through her. There was only one reason that she wanted to tell him the truth, and it wasn't because she'd suddenly come over all honest and upstanding. She'd switched places with another person—lying about who she was came with the territory. It allowed her to sit there at those excruciatingly proper dinners and try to read into King Geoffrey's facial expressions and his every word without him knowing it, still trying to figure out if she really thought he was her father. And what it would mean to her if he was. Something that would never happen if she'd identified herself. If he'd been on the defensive when he met her.

She didn't want to tell Rodolfo the truth because she had a burning desire for him to know who she was. Or she did want that, of course, but it wasn't first and foremost.

It made her stomach twist to admit it, but it was true: what she wanted was him. This. She wanted what was happening between them to be real and then, when it was, she wanted to keep him.

He is another woman's fiancé, she threw at herself in some kind of despair.

Natalie thought she'd never hated herself more than she did at that moment, because she simply couldn't seem to govern herself accordingly.

"I need to leave," she told him, and she didn't care if she sounded rude. Harsh and abrupt. She needed to remove herself from him—from all that temptation he wore entirely too easily, like another bespoke suit—before she made this all worse. Much, much worse. In ways she could imagine all too vividly. "Now."

"Princess, please. Do not run off into the night. I will only have to chase you." He moved toward her and Natalie didn't have the will to step away. To ward him off. To do what she should. And she compounded it by doing absolutely nothing when he fit his hand to her cheek and held it there. His dark eyes gleamed. "Tell me."

He was so big it made her heart hurt. The dark Roman night did nothing to obscure how beautiful he was, and she could taste him now. A kind of rich, addicting honey on her tongue. She thought that alone might make her shatter into pieces. This breath, or the next. She thought it might be the end of her.

"I need to go," she whispered, aware that her hands were in useless, desperate fists at her sides.

She wanted to punch him, she told herself, but Natalie knew that was a lie. The sad truth here was she was looking for any excuse to put her hands on him again. And she knew exactly what kind of person that made her.

And even so, she found herself leaning into that palm at her cheek.

"I never wanted what our parents had," Rodolfo told her then, his voice low and commanding, somehow, against the mild night air. "A dance in front of the cameras and nothing but duty and gritted teeth in private. I promised myself that I would marry for the right reasons. But then it seemed that what I would get instead was a cold shoulder and a polite smile. I told myself it was more than some people in my position could claim. I thought I had made my peace with it."

Natalie found she couldn't speak. As if there was a hand around her throat, gripping her much too tight.

Rodolfo didn't move any closer, though it was as

if he shut out the rest of the world. There was nothing but that near-smile on his face, that hint of light in his gaze. There was nothing but the two of them and the lie of who she was tonight, but the longer he looked at her like that, the harder it was to remember that he wasn't really hers. That he could never be hers. That none of the things he was saying to her were truly for her at all.

"Rodolfo…" she managed to say. Confession or capitulation, she couldn't tell.

"I like my name in your mouth, princess," he told her, sending heat dancing all over her, until it pooled low and hot in her belly. "And I like this. There is no reason at all we cannot take some pleasure in our solemn duty to our countries. Think of all the dreadfully tedious affairs we will enjoy a great deal more when there is this to brighten up the monotony."

His head lowered to hers again, and she wanted nothing more than to lose herself in him. In the pleasure he spoke of. In his devastating kiss, all over again.

But somehow, Natalie managed to recollect herself in the instant before his lips touched hers. She yanked herself out of his grip and stepped away from him, the night feeling cool around her now that she wasn't so close to the heat that seemed to come off him in waves.

"I'm sorry." She couldn't seem to help herself. But she kept her gaze trained on the ground, because looking at him was fraught with peril. Natalie was terribly afraid it would end only one way. "I shouldn't have…" She trailed off, helplessly. "I need to go back to my hotel."

"And do what?" he asked, and something in his voice made her stand straighter. Some kind of foreboding, perhaps. When she looked up at him, Rodolfo's gaze had gone dark again, his mouth stern and hard. "Switch personalities yet again?"

Valentina jerked as if he'd slapped her, and if he'd been a little more in control of himself, Rodolfo might have felt guilty about that.

Maybe he already did, if he was entirely honest, but he couldn't do anything about it. He couldn't reach out and put his hands on her the way he wanted to do. He couldn't do a goddamned thing when she refused to tell him what was going on.

The princess looked genuinely distraught at the thought of kissing him again. At the thought that this marriage they'd been ordered into for the good of their kingdoms could be anything but a necessary, dutiful undertaking to be suffered through for the rest of their lives.

Rodolfo didn't understand any of this. Didn't she realize that this crazy chemistry that had blazed to life out of nowhere was a blessing? The saving grace of what was otherwise nothing more than a royal chore dressed up as a photo opportunity?

Clearly she did not, because she was staring at him with something he couldn't quite read making her green eyes dark. Her lovely cheeks looked pale. She looked shaken—though that made no sense.

"What do you mean by that?" she demanded, though her voice sounded as thrown as the rest of her looked. "I have the one personality, that's all. This might come as a shock to you, I realize, but many women actually have *layers*. Many humans, in fact."

Rodolfo wanted to be soothing. He did. He prided himself on never giving in to his temper. On maintaining his cool under any and all extreme circumstances. There was no reason he couldn't calm this maddening woman, whether he understood what was going on here or not.

"Are you unwell?" he asked instead. And not particularly nicely.

"I am feeling more unwell by the moment," she threw back at him, stiff and cool. "As I told you, I need to leave."

He reached over and hooked a hand around her elbow when she made as if to turn, holding her there where she stood. Keeping her with him. And the caveman in him didn't care whether she liked it or not.

"Let go of me," she snapped at him. But she didn't pull her elbow from his grasp.

Rodolfo smiled. It was a lazy, edgy sort of smile, and he watched the color rush back into her face.

"No."

She stiffened, but she still didn't pull away. "What do you mean, *no*?"

"I mean that I have no intention of releasing you until you tell me why you blow so hot and cold, princess. And I do not much care if it takes all night. It is almost as if you are two women—"

Her green eyes flashed. "That or I find you largely unappealing."

"Until, of course, you do not find me unappealing in the least. Then you melt all over me."

Her cheeks pinkened further. "I find it as confusing as you do. Best not to encourage it, I think."

He savored the feel of her silky skin beneath his palm. "Ah, but you see, I am not confused in the least."

"If you do not let go of me, right now, I will scream," she told him.

He only smiled at her. "Go ahead. You have my blessing." He waited, and cocked an eyebrow when she only glared at him. "I thought you were about to scream down the villa, were you not? Or was that another metaphor?"

She took what looked like a shaky breath, but she didn't say anything. And she still didn't pull her elbow away. Rodolfo moved a little closer, so he could bend and get his face near hers.

"Tell me what game this is," he murmured, close to her ear. She jumped, and he expected her to pull free of him, but she didn't. She settled where she stood. He could feel her breathe. He could feel the way her pulse pounded through her. He could smell her excitement in the heated space between them, and he could feel the tension in her, too. "I am more than adept at games, I promise you. Just tell me what we're playing."

"This is no game." But her voice sounded a little broken. Just a little, but it was enough.

"When I met you, there was none of this fire," he reminded her, as impossible as that was to imagine now. "We sat through that extraordinarily painful meal—"

She tipped her head back so she could look him dead in the eye. "I loved every moment of it."

"You did not. You sat like a statue and smiled with the deepest insincerity. And then afterward, I thought you might have nodded off during my proposal."

"I was riveted." She waved the hand that wasn't trapped between them. "Your Royal Highness is all that is charming and so on. It was the high point of my life, etcetera, etcetera."

"You thanked me in your usual efficient manner, yes. But riveted?" He slid his hand down her forearm, abandoning his grip on her elbow so he could take her hand in his. Then he played with the great stone she wore on her finger that had once belonged to his grandmother and a host of Tisselian queens before her. He tugged it this way, then that. "You were anything but that, princess. You used to look through me when I spoke to you, as if I was a ghost. I could not tell if I was or you were. I imagined that I would beget my heirs on a phantom."

Something moved through her then, some electrical current that made that vulnerable mouth of hers tremble again, and she tugged her hand from his as if she'd suddenly been scalded. And yet Rodolfo felt as if he might have been, too.

"I'm not sure what the appropriate response is when a man one has agreed to marry actually sits there and explains his commitment to ongoing infidelity, as if his daily exploits in the papers were not enough of a clue. Perhaps you should count yourself lucky that all I did was look through you."

"Imagine my surprise that you noticed what I did, when you barely appeared to notice me."

"Is that what you need, Rodolfo?" she demanded, and this time, when she stepped back and completely away from him, he let her go. It seemed to startle her, and she pulled in a sharp breath as if to steady herself. "To be noticed? It may shock you to learn that the entire world already knows that, after having witnessed all your attention-seeking theatrics and escapades. That is not actually an announcement you need to make."

Rodolfo didn't exactly thrill to the way she said that, veering a bit too close to the sorts of things his father was known to hurl at him. But he admired the spirit in her while she said it. He ordered himself to concentrate on that.

"And now you are once again *this* Valentina," he replied, his voice low. "The one who dares say things to my face others would be afraid to whisper behind my back. Bold. Alluring. Who are you and what have you done with my dutiful ghost?"

She all but flinched at that and then she let out a breath that sounded a little too much like a sob. But before he could question that, she clearly swallowed it down. She lifted her chin and glared at him with nothing but sheer challenge in her eyes, and he thought he must have imagined the vulnerability in that sound she'd made. The utter loneliness.

"This Valentina will disappear soon enough, never fear," she assured him, a strange note in her voice. "We can practice that right now. I'm leaving."

But Rodolfo had no intention of letting her go. This time when she turned on her heel and walked away from him, he followed.

CHAPTER EIGHT

RODOLFO CAUGHT UP to her quickly with his long, easily athletic stride, and then refused to leave her side. He stayed too close and put his hand at the small of her back, guiding her through the splendid, sparkling crowd whether she wanted his aid or not. Natalie told herself she most emphatically did not, but just as she hadn't pulled away from him out on the terrace despite her threats that she might scream, she didn't yank herself out of his grasp now, either. She assured herself she was only thinking about what would be best for the real princess, that she was only avoiding the barest hint of scandal—but the truth was like a brand sunk deep in her belly.

She wanted him to touch her. She liked it when he did.

You are a terrible person, she told herself severely.

Natalie wanted to hate him for that, too. She told herself that of course she did, but that slick heat between her legs and the flush that she couldn't quite seem to cool let her know exactly how much of a liar she was. With every step and each shifting bit of pressure his hand exerted against her back.

He summoned their driver with a quick call, and then walked with her all the way back down the red carpet, smiling with his usual careless charm at all the paparazzi who shrieked out his name. Very much as if he enjoyed all those flashing lights and impertinent questions.

It was Natalie who wanted to curl up into a ball and hide somewhere. Natalie who wasn't used to this kind of attention—not directed at her, anyway. She'd fended off the press for Mr. Casilieris as part of her job, but she'd never been its focus before, and she discovered she really, truly didn't like it. It felt like salt on her skin. Stinging and gritty. But she didn't have the luxury of fading off into the background to catch her breath in the shadows, because she wasn't Natalie right now. She was Princess Valentina, who'd grown up with this sort of noisy spectacle everywhere she went. Who'd danced on her doting father's shoes when she was small and had cut her teeth on spotlights of all shapes and sizes and hell, for all she knew, enjoyed every moment of it the way Rodolfo seemed to.

She was Princess Valentina tonight, and a princess should have managed to smile more easily. Natalie tried her best, but by the time Rodolfo handed her into the gleaming black SUV that waited for them at the end of the press gauntlet, she thought her teeth might crack from the effort of holding her perhaps not so serene smile in place.

"I don't need your help," she told him, but it was too late. His hand was on her arm again as she clambered inside and then he was climbing in after her, forcing her to throw herself across the passenger seat or risk having him…all over her.

She hated that she had to remind herself—sternly—why that would be a bad idea.

"Would you prefer it if I had drop-kicked you into the vehicle?" he asked, still smiling as he settled himself beside her.

There was a gleam in his dark gaze that let her know he was fully aware of the way she was clinging to the far door as if it might save her. From him. As ever, he appeared not to notice the confines or restrictions of whatever he happened to be sitting on. In this case, he sprawled out in the backseat of the SUV, taking up more than his fair share of the available room and pretty much all of the oxygen. Daring her to actually come out and comment on it, Natalie was fairly sure, rather than simply twitching her skirts away from his legs in what she hoped was obvious outrage.

"I think you are well aware that neither I nor anyone else would prefer to be drop-kicked. And also that there exists yet another option, if one without any attendant theatrics. You could let me get in the car as I have managed to do all on my own for twenty-seven years and keep your hands to yourself while I did it."

He turned slightly in his seat and studied her for a

moment, as the lights of Rome gleamed behind him, streaking by in the sweet, easy dark as they drove.

"Spoken like someone who has not spent the better part of her life being helped in and out of motorcades to the roars of a besotted crowd," Rodolfo said, his dark brows high as his dark eyes took her measure. "Except you have."

Natalie could have kicked herself for making such a silly mistake, and all because she'd hoped to score a few points in their endless little battle of words. She thought she really would have given herself a pinch, at the very least, if he hadn't been watching her so closely. She sniffed instead, to cover her reaction.

"You've gone over all literal, haven't you? Back on the terrace it was all metaphor and now you're parsing what I say for any hint of exaggeration? What's next? Will you declare war on parts of speech? Set loose the Royal Tisselian Army on any grammar you dislike?"

"I am looking for hints, Valentina, but it is not figurative language that I find mysterious. It is a woman who has already changed before my eyes, more than once, into someone else."

Natalie turned her head so she could hold that stern, probing gaze of his. Steady and long. As if she really was Valentina and had nothing at all to hide.

"No one has changed before your eyes, Your Highness. I think you might have to face the fact that you are not very observant. Unless and until someone pricks at your vanity. I might as well have been a piece of furniture to you, until I mentioned I planned to let others sit on me." She let out a merry little laugh that was meant to be a slap, and hit its mark. She saw the flare of it in his gaze. "You certainly couldn't have *that*."

"Think for a moment, please." Rodolfo's voice was too dark to be truly impatient. Too rich to sound entirely frustrated. And still, Natalie braced herself. "What is the headline if I am found to be cavorting outside the bounds of holy matrimony?"

"A long, weary sigh of boredom from all sides, I'd imagine." She aimed a cool smile his way. "With a great many exclamation points."

"I am expected to fail. I have long since come to accept it is my one true legacy." Yet that dark undercurrent in his low voice and the way he lounged there, all that ruthless power simmering beneath his seeming unconcern, told Natalie that Rodolfo wasn't resigned to any such thing. "You, on the other hand? It wouldn't be *my* feelings of betrayal you would have to worry about, however unearned you might think they were. It would be the entire world that thought less of you, forever after. Is that really what you want? After you have gone to such lengths to create your spotless reputation?"

Natalie laughed again, but there was nothing funny. There was only a kind of heaviness pressing in upon her, making her feel as if she might break apart if she didn't get away from this man before something really terrible happened. Something she couldn't explain away as a latent Cinderella fantasy, lurking around inside of her without her knowledge or permission, that had put a ball and a prince together and then thrown her headfirst into an unfortunate kiss.

"What does it matter?" she asked him, aware that her voice was ragged, giving too much away—but she couldn't seem to stop herself. "There's no way out of this, so we might as well do as we like no matter what the headlines say or do not. It will make no difference. We will marry. You will have your heirs. Our kingdoms will be linked forever. Who cares about the details when that's the only part that truly matters in the long run?"

"An argument I might have made myself a month ago," Rodolfo murmured. "But we are not the people we were a month ago, princess. You must know that."

From a distance he would likely have looked relaxed. At his ease, with his legs thrust out and his collar loosened. But Natalie was closer, and she could see that glittering, dangerous thing in his gaze. She could feel it inside her, like a lethal touch of his too-talented hands, stoking fires she should have put out a long time ago.

"What I know," she managed to say over her rocketing pulse and that quickening, clenching in her core, "is that it is not I who am apparently unwell."

But Rodolfo only smiled.

Which didn't help at all.

The rest of the drive across the city was filled with

a brooding sort of silence that in many ways was worse than anything he might have said. Because the silence grew inside of her, and Natalie filled it with…images. Unhelpful images, one after the next. What might have happened if they hadn't been interrupted on that terrace, for example. Or if they'd walked a little farther into the shadows, maybe even rounding the corner so no one could see them. Would Rodolfo's hands have found their way beneath her dress again? Would they have traveled higher than her thigh—toward the place that burned the hottest for him even now?

"Thank you for the escort but I can see myself—" Natalie began when they arrived at her hotel, but Rodolfo only stared back at her in a sort of arrogant amazement that reminded her that he would one day rule an entire kingdom, no matter what the tabloids said about him now.

She restrained the little shiver that snaked down her spine, because it had nothing to do with apprehension, and let him usher her out of the car and into the hushed hotel lobby, done in sumptuous reds and deep golds and bursting with dramatic flowers arranged in stately vases. Well. It wasn't so much that she *let* him as that there was no way to stop him without causing a scene in front of all the guests in the lobby who were pretending not to gawk at them as they arrived—especially because really, yet again, Natalie didn't much *want* to stop him. Until she'd met Rodolfo, she'd never known that she was weak straight through to her core. Now she couldn't seem to remember that everywhere but here, she was known for being tough. Strong. Unflappable.

That Natalie seemed like a distant memory.

Rodolfo nodded at her security detail as he escorted her to the private, keyed elevator that led only to the penthouse suite, and then followed her into it. The door swished shut almost silently, and then it was only the two of them in a small and shiny enclosed space. Natalie braced herself, standing there just slightly behind him, with a view of his broad, high, solidly muscled back and beyond that, the gold-trimmed elevator car. She could feel the heat of him, and all that leashed danger, coming off him like flames. He surrounded her without even looking at her. He seemed to loop around her and pull tight, crushing her in his powerful grip, without so much as laying a finger upon her. She couldn't hear herself think over the thunder of her heart, the clatter of her pulse—

But nothing happened. They were delivered directly into the grand living room of the hotel's penthouse. Rodolfo stepped off and moved into the room, shrugging out of his jacket as he went. Natalie followed after him because she had no choice—or so she assured herself. It was that or go back downstairs to the hotel lobby, where she would have to explain herself to her security, the hotel staff, the other guests still sitting around with mobile phones at the ready to record her life at will.

The elevator doors slid shut behind her, and that was it. The choice was made. And it left her notably all alone in her suite's living room with the Prince she very desperately wanted to find the antithesis of charming.

There was no Roman sunset to distract her now. There was only Rodolfo, far too beautiful and much too dangerous for anyone's good. She watched the way he moved through the living room with a kind of liquid athleticism. The light from the soft lamps scattered here and there made the sprawling space feel close. Intimate.

And it made him look like some kind of god all over again. Not limned in red or gold, but draped in shadows and need.

Her throat was dry. Her lungs ached as if she'd been off running for untold miles. Her fingers trembled, and she realized she was as jittery as if she'd pulled one of her all-nighters before a big meeting and had rivers of coffee running through her veins in place of blood. It made her stomach clench tight to think that it wasn't caffeine that was messing with her tonight. It was this man before her who she should never have touched, much less kissed.

What was she going to do now?

The sad truth was, Natalie couldn't trust herself to make the right decision, or she wouldn't still be standing where she was, would she? She would have gone straight on back to her bedchamber and locked the door. She would have summoned her staff, who she knew had to be nearby, just waiting for the opportunity to serve her and usher Rodolfo out. She would have done *something* other than what she did.

Which was wait. Breathlessly. As if she really was a princess caught up in some or other enchantment. As if she could no more move a muscle than she could wave a magic wand and turn herself back into Natalie.

Rodolfo shrugged out of his jacket and tossed it over the back of one of the fussy chairs, and then he took his time turning to face her again. When he did, his dark eyes burned into her, the focused, searing hunger in them enough to send her back a step. In a wild panic or a kind of dizzy desire, she couldn't have said.

Both, something whispered inside of her. And not with any trace of fear. Not with anything the least bit like fear.

"Rodolfo," she managed to say then, in as measured a tone as she could manage, because she thought she should have been far more afraid of all those things she could feel in the air between them than she was. Either way, this was all too much. It was all temptation and need, and she could hardly think through the chaos inside of her. "This has all gotten much too fraught and strange. Why don't I have some coffee made? We can sit and talk."

"I am afraid, *princesita*, that it is much too late for talk."

He moved then. His long stride ate up the floor

and he was before her in an instant. Or perhaps it was that she didn't want to move out of his reach. She couldn't seem to make herself run. She couldn't seem to do anything at all. All she did was stand right where she was and watch him come for her, that simmering light in his dark eyes and that stern set to his mouth that made everything inside her quiver.

Maybe there was no use pretending this wasn't what she'd wanted all along. Since the very first moment she'd crossed the threshold of that reception room at the palace and discovered he was so much more than his pictures. She'd wanted to eviscerate him and instead she'd ended up on his lap with his tongue in her mouth. Had that really been by chance?

Something dark and guilty kicked inside of her at that, and she opened her mouth to protest—to do *something,* to say *anything* that might stop this—but he was upon her. And he didn't stop. Her breath left her in a rush, because he kept coming. She backed up when she thought he might collide into her, but there was nowhere to go. The doors to the elevator were at her back, closed up tight, and Rodolfo was there. *Right there.* He crowded into her. He laid a palm against the smooth metal on either side of her head and then he leaned in, trapping her between the doors of the elevator and his big, hard body.

And there was nothing but him, then. He was so much bigger than her that he became the whole world.

She could see nothing past the wall of his chest. There was no sky but his sculpted, beautiful face. And if there was a sun in the heated little sliver of space that was all he'd left between their bodies, Natalie had no doubt it would be as hot as that look in his eyes.

"I think," she began, because she had to try.

"That is the trouble. You think too much."

And then he simply bent his head and took her mouth with his.

Just like that, Natalie was lost. The delirious taste of him exploded through her, chasing fire with more fire until all she did was burn. His kiss was masterful. Slick and hot and greedy. He left absolutely no doubt as to who was in control as he took her over and sampled her, again and again, as if he'd done it a thousand times before tonight alone. As if he planned to keep doing it forever, starting now. Here.

There was no rush. No desperation or hurry. Just that endless, erotic tasting as if he could go on and on and on.

And Natalie forgot, all over again, who she was and what she was meant to be doing here.

Because she could feel him everywhere. In her fingers, her toes. In the tips of her ears and like a breeze of sensation pouring down her spine. She pushed up on her feet, high on her toes, trying to get as close to him as she could. His arms stayed braced against the elevator doors like immovable barriers, leaving her to angle herself closer. She did it without thought, grabbing hold of his soft shirt in both fists and letting the fire that burned through her blaze out of control.

Sensation stormed through her, making and remaking her as it swept along. Telling her stark truths about herself she didn't want to know. She felt flushed and wild from her lips to the tight, hard tips of her breasts, all the way to that ravenous heat between her legs.

She would have climbed him if she could. She couldn't seem to get close enough.

And then Rodolfo slowed down. His kiss turned lazy. Deep, drugging—but he made no attempt to move any closer. He kept his hands on the wall.

After several agonies of this same stalling tactic, Natalie tore her lips from his, jittery and desperate.

"Please…" she whispered.

His mouth chased hers, tipped up in the corners as he sampled her, easy and slow. Teasing her, she understood then. As if this was some kind of game, and one he could play all night long. As if she was the only one being burned to a crisp where she stood. Over and over again.

"Please, what?" he asked against her mouth, an undercurrent of laughter making her hot and furious and decidedly needy all at once. "I think you can do better than that."

"Please…" she tried again, and then lost her train of thought when his mouth found the line of her jaw.

Natalie shivered as he dropped lower, trailing fire down the side of her neck and somehow finding his way to every sensitive spot she hadn't known she had. And then he used his tongue and his teeth to taunt her with each and every one of them.

"You will have to beg," he murmured against her flushed, overwarm skin, and she could feel the rumble of his voice deep inside of her, low in her belly where all that heat seemed to bloom into a desperate softness that made her knees feel weak. "So that later, there can be no confusion, much as you may wish there to be. Beg me, *princesita.*"

Natalie told herself that she would do no such thing. Of course not. Her mother had raised a strong, tough, independent woman who did not *beg,* and especially not from a man like this. Prince Charming at his most dangerous.

But she was writhing against him. She was unsteady and wild and out of her mind, and all she wanted was his hands on her. All she wanted was *more.* And she didn't care what that made her. How could she? She hardly knew who the hell she was.

"Please, Rodolfo," she whispered, because it was the only way she could get her voice to work, that betraying little rasp. "Please, touch me."

His teeth grazed her bare shoulder, sending a wild heat dancing and spinning through her, until it shuddered into the scalding heat at her core and made everything worse.

Or better.

"I am already touching you."

"With your hands." And her voice was little more

than a moan then, which ought to have embarrassed her. But she was far beyond that. "Please."

She thought he laughed then, and she felt that, too, like another caress. It wound through her, stoking the flames and making her burn brighter, hotter. So hot she worried she might simply...explode.

And then Rodolfo dropped his arms from the wall, leaning closer to her as he did. He took her jaw in his hand and guided her mouth to his. The kiss changed, deepened, losing any semblance of laziness or control. Natalie welcomed the crush of his chest against her, the contrast between all his heat and the cool metal at her back. She wound her arms around his neck and held on to all that corded strength as he claimed her mouth over and over, as if he was as starved for her as she was for him.

She hardly dared admit how very much she wanted that to be true.

With his other hand, he reached down and began pulling up the long skirt of her dress. He took his time, plundering her mouth as he drew the hem higher and higher. She felt the faintest draft against her calf. Her knee. Then her thigh, and then his hand was on her flesh again, the way it had been that day in the palace.

Except this time, he didn't leave it one place.

He continued to kiss her, again and again, as he smoothed his way up her thigh, urging her legs apart. And Natalie felt torn in two. Ripped straight down the center by the intensity of the hunger that poured through her, then. A tumult of need and hunger and the wild flame within her that Rodolfo kept burning at a fever pitch.

When his seeking fingers reached the edge of the satiny panties she wore, he lifted his head just slightly, taking his mouth away from her. It felt like a blow. Like a loss almost too extreme to survive.

It hurts to breathe, Natalie thought dimly, still lost in the mad commotion happening everywhere in her body. Still wanting him—needing him—almost more than she could bear.

"I will make it stop," Rodolfo said, and she realized with a start that she'd spoken out loud. His mouth crooked slightly in one corner. "Eventually."

And then he dipped his fingers beneath the elastic of her panties and found the heat of her.

Natalie gasped as he stroked his way through her folds, bold and sure, directly into her softness. His other hand was at her neck, his thumb moving against her skin there the way his clever fingers played with her sex below. He traced his way around the center of her need, watching her face as she clutched at his broad wrist—but only to maintain that connection with him, not to stop him. Never that. Not now.

And then, without warning, he twisted his wrist and drove two fingers into her, that hard curve of his mouth deepening when she moaned.

"Like that, princess," he murmured approvingly. "Sing for me just like that."

And Natalie lost track of what he was doing, and how. He dropped his head to her neck again, teasing his way down to toy with the top of her bodice. He dragged his free hand over her nipples, poking hard against the fabric of the dress, and it was like lightning storming straight down the center of her body to where she was already little more than a flame. And he was stoking that fire with every thrust of his long, blunt fingers deep into her, as if he knew. As if he knew everything. Her pounding heart, that slick, impossible pleasure crashing over her, and that delicious tightening that was making her breath come too fast and too loud.

She lost herself in the slide, the heat. His wicked, talented hands and what they were doing to her. Her hips lifted of their own accord, meeting each stroke, and then the storm took her over. She let her head fall back against the elevator doors. She let herself go, delivering herself completely into his hands, as if there was nothing but this slick, insistent rhythm. As if there was nothing but the sensation he was building in her, higher and higher.

As if there was nothing left in all the world but him.

And then Rodolfo did something new, twisting his wrist and thrusting in a little bit deeper, and everything seemed to shudder to a dangerous halt. Then he did it again, and threw her straight over the edge into bliss.

Sheer, exultant bliss.

Natalie tumbled there, lost to herself and consumed by all that wondrous fire, for what seemed like a very long time.

When the world stopped spinning he was shifting her, lifting her up and into his arms. She had the vague thought that she should protest as he held her high against his chest so her head fell to his wide shoulder when she couldn't hold it up, but his gaze was dark and hungry—still so very hungry—and she couldn't seem to find her tongue to speak.

Rodolfo carried her to the long couch that stretched out before the great wall of windows with all of Rome winking and sparkling there on the other side, like some kind of dream. He laid her down carefully, as if she were infinitely precious to him, and it caught at her. It made the leftover fire still roaring inside of her bleed into…something else. Something that ached more than it should.

And that was the trouble, wasn't it?

Natalie wanted this to be real. She wanted all of this to be real. She wanted to stay Valentina forever, so it wouldn't matter what she did here because *she* would live the consequences of it. She could marry Rodolfo herself. She could—

You could lose yourself in him, a voice that sounded too much like her mother's, harsh and cold, snapped at her. It felt like a face full of cold water. *And then you could be one more thing he throws away when he gets bored. This is a man who has toys, not relationships. How can you be so foolish*

as to imagine otherwise—no matter how good he is
with his hands?

"I should have done this a long time ago," he was
saying, in a contemplative sort of way that suggested
he was talking to himself more than her. But his gaze
was so hot, so hungry. It made her shiver, deep inside, kindling the same fire she would have sworn
was already burned out. "I think it would have made
for a far better proposal of marriage, don't you?"

"Rodolfo…" she began, but he was coming down
over her on the couch. He held himself up on his
arms and gazed down at her as he settled himself
between her legs, fitting his body to hers in a way
that made them both breathe a little bit harder. Au-
dibly. And there was no pretending that wasn't real.
It made her foolish. "You may imagine you know
who I am, but you don't. You really don't."

"Quiet, *princesita*," he said in a low sort of growl
that made everything inside her, still reeling from
what he'd done with his hands alone, bloom into a
new, even more demanding sort of heat. He shifted
so he could take her face between his hands, and
that was better. Worse. Almost too intense. "I am
going to taste you again. Then I will tell you who are,
though I already know. You should know it, too." He
let his chest press against her, and dipped his chin
so his mouth was less than a gasp away. Less than
a breath. *"Mine."*

And then he set his mouth to hers and the flames
devoured her.

Again.

This time, Natalie didn't need to be told to beg for him. There was no space between them, only heat and the intense pressure of the hardest part of him, flush against her scalding heat. There was no finesse, no strategy, no teasing. Only need.

And that hunger that rolled between them like so much summer thunder.

She didn't know who undressed whom and she didn't—couldn't—care. She only knew that his mouth was a torment and a gift, both at the same time. His hands were like fire. He pulled down her bodice and feasted on the nipples he'd played with before, until Natalie was nothing but a writhing mess beneath him. Begging. Pleading. Somehow his shirt was open, and she was finally able to touch all those hard muscles she'd only imagined until now. And he was so much better than the pictures she'd seen. Hot and extraordinarily male and perfect and *here,* right here, stretched out on top of her. It was her turn to use her mouth on him, tasting the heat and salt of him until his breath was as heavy as hers, and everything was part of the same shattering, impossible magic.

At some point she wondered if it was possible to survive this much pleasure. If anyone could live through it. If she would recognize herself when this was done—but that was swept away when he took her mouth again.

She loved his weight, crushing her down into the cushions. She loved it even more when he pulled her skirts out of the way and found her panties again. This time, he didn't bother sneaking beneath them. This time he simply tugged, hard and sure, until they tore away in his hand.

And somehow that was so erotic it seemed to light her up inside. She could hardly breathe.

Rodolfo reached down and tore at his trousers, and when he shifted back into place Natalie felt him, broad and hard, nudging against her entrance. His gaze traveled over her body from the place they were joined to the skirt of the dress rucked up and twisted around her hips. Then higher, to where her breasts were plumped up above the dress's bodice, her nipples still tight and swollen from his mouth. Only then did his gaze touch her face.

Suddenly, the world was nothing but that shuddering beat of her heart, so hard she thought he must surely feel it, and that stark, serious expression he wore. He dropped down to an elbow, bringing himself closer to her.

This was happening. This was real.

He was the kind of prince she'd never dared admit she dreamed about, so big and so beautiful it hurt to be this close to him. It hurt in a way dreams never did. It ached, low and deep, and everywhere else.

"Are you ready, princess?" he asked, and his voice was another caress, rough and wild.

Natalie wanted to say something arch. Witty. Something to cut through the intensity and make her feel in control again. Anything at all that might help make this less than it was. Anything that might contain or minimize all those howling, impossible things that flooded through her then.

But she couldn't seem to open her mouth. She couldn't seem to find a single word that might help her.

Her body knew what to do without her guidance or input. As if she'd been made for this, for him. She lifted her hips and pushed herself against him, impaling herself on his hardness, one slow and shuddering inch. Then another. He muttered something in what she thought was the Spanish he sometimes used, but Natalie was caught in his dark gaze, still fast on her face.

"What are you doing to me?" he murmured. He'd asked it before.

Like then, he didn't wait for an answer. He didn't give her any warning. He wrapped an arm around her hips, then hauled them high against him. And in the next instant, slammed himself in deep.

"Oh, my God," Natalie whispered as he filled her, and everything in her shuddered again and again, nudging her so close to the edge once more that she caught her breath in anticipation.

"'Your Highness' will do," Rodolfo told her, a thread of amusement beneath the stark need in his voice.

And then he began to move.

It was a slick, devastating magic. Rodolfo built the flames in her into a wildfire, then fanned the blaze ever higher. He dropped his mouth to hers, then shifted to pull a nipple into the heat of his mouth.

Natalie wrapped herself around him, and gave herself over to each glorious thrust. She dug her fingers into his back, she let her head fall back and then she let herself go. As if the woman she'd been when she'd walked into this room, or into this life, no longer existed.

There was only Rodolfo. There was only this.

Perfect, she thought, again and again, so it became a chant inside her head. *This is perfect.*

She might even have chanted it aloud.

He dropped down closer, wrapping his arms around her as his rhythm went wilder and more erratic. He tucked his face in her neck and kept his mouth there as he pounded into her, over and over, until he hurled her straight back off that cliff.

And he followed her only moments later, releasing himself into her with a roar that echoed through the room and deep inside of Natalie, too, tearing her apart in a completely different way as reality slammed back into her, harsh and cruel.

Because she'd never felt closer to a man in all her life, and Rodolfo had called out to her as if he felt the same. She was as certain as she'd ever been of anything that he felt exactly the same as she did.

But, of course, he thought she was someone else.

And he'd used the wrong name.

CHAPTER NINE

RODOLFO HAD BARELY shifted his weight from Valentina before she was rolling out from beneath him, pulling the voluminous skirt of her dress with her as she climbed to her feet. He found he couldn't help but smile. She was so unsteady on her feet that she had to reach out and grab hold of the nearby chair to keep from sagging to the ground.

He was male enough to find that markedly satisfying.

"You are even beautiful turned away from me," he told her without meaning to speak. It was not, generally, his practice to traffic in flattery. Mostly because it was never required. But it was the simple truth as far as Valentina was concerned. Not empty flattery at all.

She shivered slightly, as if in reaction to his words, but that was all. She didn't glance back at him. She was pulling her dress back into place, shaking back her hair that had long since tumbled from its once sleek chignon. And all Rodolfo wanted to do was pull her back down to him. He wanted to indulge himself and take a whole lot more time with her. He wanted to strip her completely and make sure he learned every last inch of her sweet body by heart.

He was more than a little delighted at the prospect of a long life together to do exactly that.

Rodolfo zipped himself up and rolled to a sitting position, aware that he felt lighter than he had in a long time. Years.

Since Felipe died.

Because the truth was, he'd never wanted his brother's responsibilities. He'd wanted his brother. Funny, irreverent, remarkably warm Felipe had been Rodolfo's favorite person for the whole of his life, and then he'd died. So suddenly. So needlessly. He'd locked himself in his rooms to sleep through what he'd assumed was a flu, and he'd been gone within the week. There was a part of Rodolfo that would never accept that. That never had. That would grieve his older brother forever.

But Rodolfo was the Crown Prince of Tissely now no matter how he grieved his brother, and that meant he should have had all of the attendant responsibilities whether he liked it or not. His father had felt otherwise. And every year the king failed to let Rodolfo take Felipe's place in his court and his government was like a slap in the face all over again, of course. It was a very public, very deliberate rebuke.

More than that, it confirmed what Rodolfo had always known to be true. He could not fill Felipe's shoes. He could not come anywhere close and that would never change. There was no hope.

Until now, he'd assumed that was simply how it would be. His father would die at some point, having allowed Rodolfo no chance at all to figure out his role as king. Rodolfo would have to do it on the fly, which was a terrific way to plunge a country straight into chaos. It was one of the reasons he'd dedicated himself to the sort of sports that required a man figure out how to remain calm no matter what was coming at him. Sharks. The earth, many thousands of feet below, at great speed. Assorted impossible mountain peaks that had killed many men before him. He figured it was all good practice for the little gift his father planned to leave him, since he suspected the old man was doing his level best to ensure that all his dire predictions about the kind of king Rodolfo would be would come true within days of his own death.

This engagement was a test, nothing more. Rodolfo had no doubt that his father expected him to fail, somehow, at an arranged marriage that literally required nothing of him save that he show up. And perhaps he'd played into that, by continuing to see other women and doing nothing to keep that discreet.

But everything was different now. Valentina was his. And their marriage would be the kind of real union Rodolfo had always craved. Without even meaning to, Rodolfo had beaten his father at the old man's own cynical little game.

And it was more than that. Rodolfo had to believe that if he could make the very dutiful princess his the way he had tonight, if he could take a bloodless royal arrangement and make it a wildfire of a marriage, he could do anything. Even convince his dour father to see him as more than just an unwelcome replacement for his beloved lost son.

For the first time in a long, long while, Rodolfo felt very nearly *hopeful*.

"Princess," he began, reaching out to wrap a hand around her hip and tug her toward him, because she was still showing him her back and he wanted her lovely face, "you must—"

"Stop calling me that!" she burst out, sounding raw. And something like wild.

She twisted out of his grasp. And he was so surprised by her outburst that he let her go.

Valentina didn't stop moving until she'd cleared the vast glass table set before the couch, and then she stood there on the other side, her chest heaving as if she'd run an uphill mile to get there.

His princess did not look anything like *hopeful*. If anything, she looked… Wounded. Destroyed. Rodolfo couldn't make any sense out of it. Her green eyes were dark and that sweet, soft mouth of hers trembled as if the hurt inside her was on the verge of pouring out even as she stood there before him.

"I can't believe I let this happen…" she whispered, and her eyes looked full. Almost blank with an anguish Rodolfo couldn't begin to understand.

Rodolfo wanted to stand, to go to her, to offer her what comfort he could—but something stopped him. How many times would she do this back and forth in one way or another? How many ways would she find to pull the rug out from under him—and as he thought that, it was not lost on Rodolfo that unlike every other woman he'd ever known, he cared a little too deeply about what this one was about. All this melodrama and for what? There was no stopping their wedding or the long, public, political marriage that would follow. It was like a train bearing down on them and it always had been.

From the moment Felipe had died and Rodolfo had been sat down and told that in addition to losing his best friend he now had a different life to live than the one he'd imagined he would, there had been no deviating from the path set before them. Princess Valentina had already been his—entirely his—before he'd laid a single finger on her. What had happened here only confirmed what had always been true, not that there had been any doubt. Not for him, anyway.

The only surprise was how much he wanted her. Again, now, despite the fact he'd only just had her. She made him…thirsty in a way he'd never experienced before in his life.

But it wouldn't have mattered if she'd stayed the same pale, distant ghost he'd met at their engagement celebration. The end result—their marriage and all the politics involved—would have been the same.

He didn't like to see her upset. He didn't like it at all. It made his jaw clench tight and every muscle in his body go much too taut. But Rodolfo remained where he was.

"If you mean what happened right here—" and he nodded at the pillow beside him as if could play back the last hour in vivid color "—then I feel I must tell you that it was always going to happen. It was only a question of when. Before the wedding or after it. Or did you imagine heirs to royal kingdoms were delivered by stork?"

But it was as if she couldn't hear him. "Why didn't you let me leave the gala alone?"

He shrugged, settling back against the pillows as if he was entirely at his ease, though he was not. Not at all. "I assume that was a rhetorical question, as that was never going to happen. You can blame the unfortunate optics if you must. But there was no possibility that my fiancée was ever going to sneak out of a very public event on her own, leaving me behind. How does that suit our narrative?"

"I don't care about your narrative."

"*Our* narrative, Valentina, and you should. You will. It is a weapon against us or a tool we employ. The choice is ours."

She was frowning now, and it was aimed at him, yet Rodolfo had the distinct impression she was talking to herself. "You should never, ever have come up here tonight."

He considered her for a moment. "This was not a mistake, *princesita*. This was a beginning."

She lifted her hands to her face and Rodolfo saw that they were shaking. Again, he wanted to go to her and again, he didn't. It was something about the stiff way she was standing there, or what had looked like genuine torment on her face before she'd covered it from his view. It gripped him, somehow, and kept him right where he was.

As if, he realized in the next moment, he was waiting for the other shoe to drop. The way he had been ever since he'd discovered at too young an age that anything and anyone could be taken from him with no notice whatsoever.

But that was ridiculous. There was no "other shoe" here. This was an arranged marriage set up by their fathers when Valentina was a baby. One crown prince of Tissely and one princess of Murin, and the kingdoms would remain forever united. Two small countries who, together, could become a force to be reckoned with in these confusing modern times. The contracts had been signed for months. They were locked into this wedding no matter what, with no possibility of escape.

Rodolfo knew. He'd read every line of every document that had required his signature. And still, he didn't much like that thing that moved him, dark and grim, as he watched her. It felt far too much like foreboding.

His perfect princess, who had just given herself

to him with such sweet, encompassing heat that he could still feel the burn of it all over him and through him as if he might feel it always, dropped her hands from her face. Her gaze caught his and held. Her eyes were still too dark, and filled with what looked like misery.

Sheer, unmistakable misery. It made his chest feel tight.

"I should never have let any of this happen," she said, and her voice was different. Matter-of-fact, if hollow. She swallowed, still keeping her eyes trained on his. "This is my fault. I accept that."

"Wonderful," Rodolfo murmured, aware his voice sounded much too edgy. "I do so enjoy being blameless. It is such a novelty."

She clenched her hands together in front of her, twisting her fingers together into a tangle. There was something about the gesture that bothered him, though he couldn't have said what. Perhaps it was merely that it seemed the very antithesis of the sort of thing a woman trained since birth to be effortlessly graceful would do. No matter the provocation.

"I am not Princess Valentina."

He watched her say that. Or rather, he saw her lips move and he heard the words that came out of her mouth, but they made no sense.

Her mouth, soft and scared, pressed into a line. "My name is Natalie."

"Natalie," he repeated, tonelessly.

"I ran into the princess in, ah—" She cleared her

throat. "In London. We were surprised, as you might imagine, to see…" She waved her hand in that way of hers, as if what she was saying was reasonable. Or even possible. Instead of out-and-out gibberish. "And it seemed like a bit of a lark, I suppose. I got to pretend to be a princess for a bit. What could be more fun? No one was ever meant to know, of course."

"I beg your pardon." He still couldn't move. He thought perhaps he'd gone entirely numb, but he knew, somehow, that the paralytic lack of feeling was better than what lurked on the other side. Much better. "But where, precisely, is the real princess in this ludicrous scenario?"

"Geographically, do you mean? She's back in London. Or possibly Spain, depending."

"All tucked up in whatever your life is, presumably." He nodded as if that idiocy made sense. "What did you say your name was, again?"

She looked ill at ease. As well she should. "Natalie."

"And if your profession is not that of the well-known daughter of a widely renowned and ancient royal family, despite your rather remarkable likeness to Princess Valentina, dare I ask what is it that you do? Does it involve a stage, perhaps, the better to hone these acting skills?"

"I'm a personal assistant. To a very important businessman."

"A jumped-up secretary for a man in trade. Of course." He was getting less numb by the second, and that was no good for anyone—though Rodolfo found he didn't particularly care. He hadn't lost his temper in a long while, but these were extenuating circumstances, surely. She should have been grateful he wasn't breaking things. He shook his head, and even let out a laugh, though nothing was funny. "I must hand it to you. Stage or no stage, this has been quite an act."

She blinked. "Somehow, that doesn't sound like a compliment."

"It was really quite ingenious. All you had to do was walk in the room that day and actually treat me like another living, breathing human instead of a cardboard cutout. After all those months. You must have been thrilled that I fell into your trap so easily."

The words felt sour in his own mouth. But Valentina only gazed back at him with confusion written all over her, as if she didn't understand what he was talking about. He was amazed that he'd fallen for her performance. Why hadn't it occurred to him that her public persona, so saintly and retiring, was as much a constriction as his daredevil reputation? As easily turned off as on. And yet it had never crossed his mind that she was anything but the woman she'd always seemed to be, hailed in all the papers as a paragon of royal virtue. A breath of fresh air, they called her. The perfect princess in every respect.

He should have known that all of it was a lie. A carefully crafted, meticulously built lie.

"The trap?" She was shaking her head, looking

lost and something like forlorn, and Rodolfo hated that even when he knew she was trying to play him, he still wanted to comfort her. Get his hands on her and hold her close. It made his temper lick at him, dark and dangerous. "What trap?"

"All of this so you could come back around tonight and drop this absurd story on me. Did you really think I would credit such an outlandish tale? You *happen* to resemble one of the wealthiest and most famous women in the world, yet no one remarked on this at any point during your other life. Until, by chance, you stumbled upon each other. How convenient. And that day in the palace, when you came back from London—am I meant to believe that you had never met me before?"

She pressed her lips together as if aware that they trembled. "I hadn't."

"What complete and utter rubbish." He stood then, smoothing his shirt down as he rose to make sure he kept his damned twitchy hands to himself, but there wasn't much he could do about the fury in his voice. "I am not entirely certain which part offends me more. That you would go to the trouble to concoct such a childish, ridiculous story in the first place, or that you imagined for one second that I would believe it."

"You said yourself that I was switching personalities. That I was two women. This is why. I think—I mean, the only possible explanation is that Valentina and I are twins." There was an odd emphasis on that last word, as if she'd never said it out loud before. She squared her shoulders. "Twin sisters."

Rodolfo fought to keep himself under control, despite the ugly things that crawled through him then, each worse than the last. The truth was, he should have known better than to be hopeful. About anything. He should have known better than to allow himself to think that anything in his life might work out. He could jump out of a thousand planes and land safely. There had never been so much as a hiccup on any of his adventures, unless he counted the odd shark bite or scar. But when it came to his actual life as a prince of Tissely? The things he was bound by blood and his birthright to do whether he wanted to or not? It was nothing but disaster, every time.

He should have known this would be, too.

"Twin sisters," he echoed when he trusted himself to speak in both English and a marginally reasonable tone. "But I think you must mean *secret* twin sisters, to give it the proper soap opera flourish. And how do you imagine such a thing could happen? Do you suppose the king happily looked the other way while Queen Frederica swanned off with a stolen baby?"

"No one talks about where she went. Much less who she went with."

"You are talking about matters of state, not idle gossip." His hands were in fists, and he forced them to open, then shoved them in his pockets. "The queen's mental state was precarious. Everyone knows this.

She would hardly have been allowed to retreat so completely from public life with a perfectly healthy child who also happened to be one of the king's direct heirs."

Valentina frowned. "Precarious? What do you mean?"

"Do not play these games with me," he gritted out, aware that his heart was kicking at him. Temper or that same, frustrated hunger, he couldn't tell. "You know as well as I do that she was not assassinated, no matter how many breathless accounts are published in the dark and dingy corners of the internet by every conspiracy theorist who can type. That means, for your story to make any kind of sense, a king with no other heirs in line for his throne would have to release one of the two he did have into the care of a woman who was incapable of fulfilling a single one of her duties as his queen. Or at the very least, somehow fail to hunt the world over for the child once this same woman stole her."

"I didn't really think about that part," she said tightly. "I was more focused on the fact I was in a palace and the man with the crown was acting as if he was my father. Which it turns out, he probably is."

"Enough." He belted it out at her, with enough force that her head jerked back a little. "The only thing this astonishing conversation is doing is making me question your sanity. You must know that." He let out a small laugh at that, though it scraped at him. "Perhaps that is your endgame. A mental breakdown or two, like mother, like daughter. If you cannot get out of the marriage before the wedding, best to start working on how to exit it afterward, I suppose."

Her face was pale. "That's not what this is. I'm trying to be honest with you."

He moved toward her then, feeling his lips thin as he watched her fight to stand her ground when she so clearly wanted to put more furniture between them—if not whole rooms.

"Have I earned this, Valentina?" he demanded, all that numbness inside him burning away with the force of his rage. His sense of betrayal—which he didn't care to examine too closely. It was enough that she'd led him to hope, then kicked it out of his reach. It was more than enough. "That you should go to these lengths to be free of me?"

He stopped when he was directly in front of her, and he hated the fact that even now, all he wanted to do was pull her into his arms and kiss her until the only thing between them was that heat. Her eyes were glassy and she looked pale with distress, and he fell for it. Even knowing what she was willing to do and say, his first instinct was to believe her. What did that say about his judgment?

Maybe his father had been right about him all along.

That rang in him like a terrible bell.

"Here is the sad truth, princess," he told her, standing above her so she was forced to tilt her head back to keep her eyes on him. And his body didn't know that everything had changed, of course. It was far more straightforward. It wanted her, no matter what stories she told. "There is no escape. There is no sneaking away into some fantasy life where you will live out your days without the weight of a country or two squarely on your shoulders. There is no switching places with a convenient twin and hiding from who you are. And I am terribly afraid that part of what you must suffer is our marriage. You are stuck with me. Forever."

"Rodolfo." And her voice was scratchy, as if she had too many sobs in her throat. As if she was fighting to hold them back. "I know it all sounds insane, but you have to listen to me—"

"No," he said with quiet ferocity. "I do not."

"Rodolfo—"

And now even his name in her mouth felt like an insult. Another damned lie. He couldn't bear it.

He silenced her the only way he knew how. He reached out and hooked a hand around her neck, dragging her to him. And then he claimed her mouth with his.

Rodolfo poured all of the dark things swirling around inside of him into the way he angled his jaw to make everything bright hot and slick. Into the way he took her. Tasted her. As if she was the woman he'd imagined she was, so proper and bright. As if he could still taste that fantasy version of her now despite the games she was trying to play. He gave her his grief over Felipe, his father's endless shame and fury that the wrong son had died—all of it. If she'd taken away his hope, he could give her the rest of it. He kissed her again and again, as much a penance for him as any kind of punishment for her.

And when he was done, because it was that or he would take her again right there on the hotel floor and he wasn't certain either one of them would survive that, he set her away from him.

It should have mattered to him that she was breathing too hard. That her green eyes were wide and there were tears marking her cheeks. It should have meant something.

Somewhere, down below the tumult of that black fury that roared in him, inconsolable and much too wounded, it did. But he ignored it.

"I only wanted you to know who I am," she whispered.

And that was it, then. That was too much. He took her shoulders in his hands and dragged her before him, up on her toes and directly in his face.

"I am Rodolfo of Tissely," he growled at her. "The accidental, throwaway prince. I was called *the spare* when I was born, always expected to live in my brother's shadow and never, ever expected to take Felipe's place. Then the spare became the heir—but only in name. Because I have always been the bad seed. I have always been unworthy."

"That's not true."

He ignored her, his fingers gripping her and keeping her there before him. "Nothing I touch has ever lasted. No one I love has ever loved me back, or if they did, it was only as long as there were two sons instead of the one. Or they disappeared into the wilds of Bavaria, pretending to be ill. Or they died of bloody sepsis in the middle of a castle filled with royal doctors and every possible medication under the sun."

She whispered his name as if she loved him, and that hurt him worse than all the rest. Because more than all the rest, he wanted that to be true—and he knew exactly how much of a fool that made him.

"What is one more princess who must clearly hate the very idea of me, the same as all the rest?" And what did it matter that he'd imagined that she might be the saving of him, of the crown he'd never wanted and the future he wasn't prepared for? "None of this matters. You should have saved your energy. This will all end as it was planned. The only difference is that now, I know exactly how deceitful you are. I know the depths of the games you will play. And I promise you this, princess. You will not fool me again."

"You don't understand," she said, more tears falling from her darkened green eyes as she spoke and wetting her pale cheeks. "I wanted this to be real, Rodolfo. I lost myself in that."

He told himself to let go of her. To take his hand off her shoulders and step away. But he didn't do it. If anything, he held her tighter. Closer.

As if he'd wanted it to be real, too. As if some part of him still did.

"You have to believe me," she whispered. "I never meant it to go that far."

"It was only sex," he told her, his voice a thing of granite. He remembered what she'd called herself as she'd spun out her fantastical little tale. "But no need to worry, *Natalie*." She flinched, and he was bastard enough to like that. Because he wanted her to hurt, too—and no matter that he hated himself for that thought. Hating himself didn't change a thing. It never had. "I will be certain to make you scream while we make the requisite heirs. I am nothing if not dependable in that area, if nowhere else. Feel free to ask around for references."

He let her go then, not particularly happy with how hard it was to do, and headed for the elevator. He needed to clear his head. He needed to wash all of this away. He needed to find a very dark hole and fall into it for a while, until the self-loathing receded enough that he could function again. Assuming it ever would.

"It doesn't have to be this way," she said from behind him.

But Rodolfo turned to face her only when he'd stepped into the elevator. She stood where he'd left her, her hands tangled in front of her again and something broken in her gaze.

Eventually, she would have as little power over him as she'd had when they'd met. Eventually, he would not want to go to her when she looked at him like that, as if she was small and wounded and only he could heal her. *Eventually.* All he had to do was survive long enough to get there, like anything else.

"It can only be this way," he told her then, and he hardly recognized his own voice. He sounded like a broken man—but of course, that wasn't entirely true. He had never been whole to begin with. "The sooner you resign yourself to it, the better. I am very much afraid this is who we are."

Natalie didn't move for a long, long time after Rodolfo left. If she could have turned into a pillar of stone, she would have. It would have felt better, she was sure.

The elevator doors shut and she heard the car move, taking Rodolfo away, but she still stood right where he'd left her as if her feet were nailed to the floor. Her cheeks were wet and her dress caught at her since she'd pulled it back into place in such a panicked hurry, and her fingers ached from where she'd threaded them together and held them still. Her breathing had gone funny because her throat was so tight.

And for a long while, it seemed that the only thing she could do about any of those things was stay completely still. As if the slightest movement would make it all worse—though it was hard to imagine how.

Eventually, her fingers began to cramp, and she unclasped them, then shook them out. After that it was easier to move the rest of her. She walked on stiff, protesting legs down the long penthouse hallway into her bedroom, where she stood for a moment in the shambles of her evening, blind to the luxury all around her. But that could only last so long. She went to kick off her shoes and realized she'd lost them somewhere, but she didn't want to go back out to the living room and look. She was sure Rodolfo's contempt was still clinging to every gleaming surface out there and she couldn't bring herself to face it.

She padded across the grandly appointed space to the adjoining bathroom suite and stepped in to find the bath itself was filled and waiting for her, steam rising off the top of the huge, curved, freestanding tub like an invitation. That simple kindness made her eyes fill all over again. She wiped the blurriness away, but it didn't help, and the tears were flowing freely again by the time she got herself out of her dress and threw it over a chair in the bedroom. She didn't cry. She almost never cried. But tonight she couldn't seem to stop.

Natalie returned to the bathroom to pull all the pins out of her hair. She piled the mess of it on her head and knotted it into place, ignoring all the places she felt stiff or sore. Then she walked across the marble floor and climbed into the tub at last, sinking into the warm, soothing embrace of the bath's hot water and the salts that some kind member of the staff had thought to add.

She closed her eyes and let herself drift—but then

there was no more hiding from the events of the night. The dance. That kiss out on the terrace of the villa. And then what had happened right here in this hotel. His mouth against her skin. His wickedly clever hands. The bold, deep surge of his possession and how she'd fallen to pieces so easily. The smile on Rodolfo's face when he'd turned her around to face him afterward, and how quickly it had toppled from view. And that shuttered, haunted look she'd put in his eyes later, that had been there when he'd left.

As if that was all that remained of what had swelled and shimmered between them tonight. As if that was all it had ever been.

Whatever else came of these stolen days here in Valentina's life, whatever happened, Natalie knew she would never forgive herself for that. For believing in a fairy tale when she knew better and hurting Rodolfo—to say nothing of herself—in the process.

She sat in the tub until her skin was shriveled and the water had cooled. She played the night all the way through, again and again, one vivid image after the next. And when she sat up and pulled the plug to let the water swirl down the drain, she felt clean, yes. But her body didn't feel like hers. She could still feel Rodolfo's touch all over, as if he'd branded her with his passion as surely as he'd condemned her with his disbelief.

Too bad, she told herself, sounding brisk and hard like her mother would have. *This is what you get for doing what you knew full well you shouldn't have.*

Natalie climbed out of the tub then and wrapped herself in towels so light and airy they could have been clouds, but she hardly noticed. She stood in the still-fogged-up bathroom and brushed out her hair, letting the copper strands fall all around her like a curtain and then braiding the heavy mess of it to one side, so she could toss it over one shoulder and forget it.

When she walked back into the bedroom, her dress was gone from the chair where she'd thrown it and in its place was the sort of silky thing Valentina apparently liked to sleep in. Natalie had always preferred a simple T-shirt, but over the past couple of weeks she'd grown to like the sensuous feel of the fine silk against her bare skin.

Tonight, however, it felt like a rebuke.

Her body didn't want silk, it wanted Rodolfo.

She would have given anything she had to go back in time and keep herself from making that confession. To accept that of course he would call her by the wrong name and find a way to make her peace with it. Her mind spun out into one searing fantasy after another about how the night would have gone if only she'd kept her mouth shut.

But that was the trouble, wasn't it? She'd waited too long to tell him the truth, if she was going to. And she never should have allowed him to touch her while he thought she was Valentina. Not back in the palace. Certainly not tonight. She should have kept her distance from him entirely.

Because no matter what her traitorous heart insisted, even now, he wasn't hers. He could never be hers. The ring on her finger belonged to another woman and so did he. It didn't matter that Valentina had given her blessing, whatever that meant in the form of a breezy text. Natalie had never wanted to be the sort of woman who took another woman's man, no matter the circumstances. She'd spent her whole childhood watching her mother flit from one lover to the next, knowing full well that many of the men Erica juggled had been married already. Natalie always vowed that she was not going to be one of those women who pretended they didn't know when a man was already committed elsewhere. In this case, she'd known going in and she'd still ended up here.

How many more ways was she going to betray herself?

How many more lives was she going to ruin besides her own?

Natalie looked around the achingly gorgeous room, aware of every last detail that made it the perfect room for a princess, from the soaring canopy over her high, proud bed to the deep Persian rugs at her feet. The epic sweep of the drapery at each window and the stunning view of Rome on the other side of the glass. The artistry in every carved leg of each of the chairs placed *just so* at different points around the chamber. She looked down at her own body, still warm and pink from her bath and barely covered in a flowy, bright blue silk that cascaded lazily from two spaghetti straps at her shoulders. Her manicure and pedicure were perfect. Her skin was as soft as a baby's after access to Valentina's moisturizing routine with products crafted especially for her. Her hair had never looked so shiny or healthy, even braided over one shoulder. And she was wearing nothing but silk and a ring fit for a queen. Literally.

But she didn't belong here with these things that would never belong to her. She might fit into this borrowed life in the most physical sense, but none of it suited her. *None of it was hers.*

"I am Natalie Monette," she told herself fiercely, her own voice sounding loud and brash in the quiet of the room. Not cool and cultured, like a princess. "My fingernails are never painted red. My toes are usually a disaster. I live on pots of coffee and fistfuls of ibuprofen, not two squares of decadent chocolate a day and healthy little salads."

She moved over to the high bed, where Valentina's laptop and mobile phone waited for her on a polished bedside table, plugged in and charged up, because not even that was her responsibility here.

It was time to go home. It was time to wake up from this dream and take back what was hers—her career—before she lost that, too.

It was time to get back to the shadows, where she belonged.

She picked up the mobile and punched in her own number, telling herself this would all fade away fast when she was back in her own clothes and her own life. When she had too much to do for Mr. Casilieris to waste her time brooding over a prince she'd never see again. Soon this little stretch of time would be like every other fairy tale she'd ever been told as a girl, a faded old story she might recall every now and then, but no part of anything that really mattered to her.

And so what if her heart seemed to twist at that, making her whole chest ache?

It was still time—past time—to go back where she belonged.

"I am Natalie Monette," she whispered to herself as the phone on the other end rang and rang. "I am not a princess. I was never a princess and I never will be."

But it didn't matter what she told herself, because Valentina didn't answer.

Not that night.

And not for weeks.

CHAPTER TEN

RODOLFO WAS CONFLICTED.

He hadn't seen Valentina since that night in Rome. He'd had his staff contact her to announce that he thought they'd carried out their objectives beautifully and there would be no more need for their excursions into the world of the paparazzi. And that was before he'd seen their pictures in all the papers.

The one most prominently featured showed the two of them on the dance floor, in the middle of what looked like a very romantic waltz. Rodolfo was gazing down at her as if he had never seen a woman before in all his life. That was infuriating enough, given what had come afterward. It made his chest feel too tight. But it was the look on the princess's face that had rocked Rodolfo.

Because the picture showed her staring up at the man who held her in his arms in open adoration. As if she was falling in love right then and there as they danced. As if it had already happened.

And it had all been a lie. A game.

The first you've ever lost, a vicious voice inside of him whispered.

Today he stood in the grand foyer outside his father's offices in the palace in Tissely, but his attention was across Europe in Murin, where the maddening, still-more-fascinating-than-she-should-have-been woman who was meant to become his wife was going about her business as if she had not revealed herself to be decidedly unhinged.

She'd kept a low profile these last few weeks. As had Rodolfo.

But his fury hadn't abated one bit.

Secret twins. The very idea was absurd—even if she hadn't been the daughter of one of the most famous and closely watched men in the world. There was press crawling all over Murin Castle day and night and likely always had been, especially when the former queen had been pregnant with the heir to the country's throne.

"Ridiculous," he muttered under his breath.

But his trouble was, he didn't want to be bitter. He wanted to believe her, no matter how unreasonable she was. That was what had been driving him crazy these past weeks. He'd told himself he was going to throw himself right back into his old habits, but he hadn't. Instead he'd spent entirely too much time mired in his old, familiar self-pity and all it had done was make him miss her.

He had no earthly idea what to do about that.

The doors opened behind him and he was led in

with the usual unnecessary ceremony to find his father standing behind his desk. Already frowning, which Rodolfo knew from experience didn't bode well for the bracing father/son chat they were about to have.

Ferdinand nodded at the chair before his desk and Rodolfo took it, for once not flinging himself down like a lanky adolescent. Not because doing so always irritated his father. But because he felt like a different man these days, scraped raw and hollow and made new in a variety of uncomfortable and largely unpleasant ways he could blame directly on his princess, and he didn't have it in him to needle his lord and king whenever possible.

His father's frown deepened as he beheld his son before him, because, of course, he always had it in him to poke at his son. It was an expression Rodolfo knew well. He had no idea why it was harder to keep his expression impassive today.

"I hope you have it in you to acquit yourself with something more like grace at your wedding," Ferdinand said darkly, as if Rodolfo had been rousted out of a den of iniquity only moments before and still reeked of excess. He'd tried. In the sense that he'd planned to go out and drown himself in all the things that had always entertained him before. But he'd never made it out. He couldn't call it fidelity to his lying, manipulative princess when the truth was, he'd lost interest in sin—could he? "The entire world will be watching."

"The entire world has been watching for some time," Rodolfo replied, keeping his tone easy. Even polite. Because there was no need to inform his father that he had no intention of marrying a woman who had tried to play him so thoroughly. How could he? But he told himself Ferdinand could find out when he didn't appear at the ceremony, like everyone else. "Has that not been the major point of contention all these years?"

His father ignored him. "It is one thing to wave at a press call. Your wedding to the Murin princess will be one of the most-watched ceremonies in modern Europe. Your behavior must, at last, be that of a prince of Tissely. Do you think you can manage this, Rodolfo?"

He glared at him as if he expected an answer. And something inside of Rodolfo simply...cracked.

It was so loud that first he thought it was the chair beneath him, but his father didn't react. And it took Rodolfo a moment to understand that it wasn't his chair. It was him.

He died, Rodolfo, his princess had said in Rome, before she'd revealed herself. *You lived.*

And he'd tried so hard to reverse that, hadn't he? He'd told himself all these years that the risks he took were what made him feel alive, but that had been a lie. What he'd been doing was punishing himself. Pushing himself because he hadn't cared what happened to him. Risking himself because he'd been without hope.

Until now.

"I am not merely *a* prince of Tissely," he said with a great calm that seemed to flood him then, the way it always did before he dropped from great heights with only a parachute or threw himself off the sides of bridges and ravines attached to only a bouncy rope. Except this time he knew the calm was not a precursor to adrenaline, but to the truth. At last. "I am the only prince of Tissely."

"I know very well who you are," his father huffed at him.

"Do you, sir? Because you have seemed to be laboring under some misconceptions as to my identity this last decade or two."

"I am your father and your king," his father thundered.

But Rodolfo was done being put into his place. He was done accepting that his place was somehow lower and shameful, for that matter.

All he'd done was live. Imperfectly and often foolishly, but he'd lived a life. He might have been lying to himself. He might have been hopeless. But he'd survived all of that.

The only thing he was guilty of was of not being Felipe.

"I am your son," Rodolfo replied, his voice like steel. "I am your only remaining son and your only heir. It doesn't matter how desperately you cling to your throne. It doesn't matter how thoroughly you convince yourself that I am worthless and undeserving. Even if it were true, it wouldn't matter. Nothing you do will ever bring Felipe back."

His father looked stiff enough to break in half. And old, Rodolfo thought. How had he missed that his father had grown old? "How dare you!"

He was tired of this mausoleum his father had built around Felipe's memory. He was tired of the games they played, two bitter, broken men who had never recovered from the same long-ago loss and instead, still took it out on each other.

Rodolfo was done with the game. He didn't want to live like this any longer.

He wanted to feel the way he did when he was with Valentina. Maybe it had all been a lie, but he'd been *alive.* Not putting on a show. Not destined to disappoint simply by showing up.

And there was something he should have said a decade or two ago.

"I am all you have, old man." He stood then, taking his time and never shifting his gaze from his father's, so perhaps they could both take note of the fact that he towered over the old man. "Whether you like it or do not, I am still here. Only one of your sons died all those years ago. And only you can decide if you will waste the rest of your life acting as if you lost them both."

His father was not a demonstrative man. Ferdinand stood like a stone for so long that Rodolfo thought he might stand like that forever. So committed to the mausoleum he'd built that he became a part of it in fact.

But Rodolfo wanted no part of it. Not anymore. He was done with lies. With games. With paying over and over for sins that were not his.

He inclined his head, then turned for the door. He was reaching for the knob to let himself out—to leave this place and get on with his life—when he heard a faint noise from behind him.

"It is only that I miss him," came his father's voice, low and strained. It was another man's sob.

Rodolfo didn't turn around. It would embarrass them both.

"I know, Papa," he said, using a name he hadn't thought, much less spoken aloud, since he was little more than a baby himself. But it was the only one that seemed appropriate. "I do, too."

The first week after that shattering trip to Rome, Natalie tried Valentina so many times she was slightly afraid it would have bordered on harassment—had she not been calling her own mobile number. And it didn't matter anyway, because the princess never answered, leaving Natalie to sit around parsing the differences between a ringing phone that was never picked up and a call that went straight to voice mail like an adolescent girl worrying over a boy's pallid attentions.

And in the meantime, she still had to live Valentina's life.

That meant endless rounds of charity engagements. It meant approximately nine million teas with the ladies of this or that charity and long, sad walks through hospitals filled with ill children. It was being expected to "say a few words" at the drop of a hat, and always in a way that would support the crown while offending no one. It meant dinners with King Geoffrey, night after night, that she gradually realized were his version of preparing Valentina for the role she would be expected to fill once she married and was the next Queen of Tissely. It also meant assisting in the planning of the impending royal wedding, which loomed larger with every day that passed.

Every call you don't answer is another questionable decision I'm making for YOUR wedding, she texted Valentina after a particularly long afternoon of menu selecting. I hope you enjoy the taste of tongue and tripe. Both will feature prominently.

But the princess didn't respond.

Which meant Natalie had no choice but to carry on playing Valentina. She supposed she could fly to London and see if she was there, but the constant stream of photographs screeching about her *fairy-tale love affair* in the papers made her think that turning up at Achilles Casilieris's property this close to Valentina's wedding would make everything worse. It would cause too much commotion.

It would make certain that when they finally did switch, Natalie wouldn't be able to seamlessly slip back into her old life.

Meanwhile, everything was as Rodolfo had predicted. The public loved them, and the papers dutifully recycled the same pictures from Rome again and again. Sometimes there were separate shots of them going about their business in their separate countries, and Natalie was more than a little embarrassed by the fact she pored over the pictures of Rodolfo like any obsessed tabloid reader. One day the papers were filled with stories about how daredevil, playboy Rodolfo encouraged Valentina to access her playful side, bringing something real and rare to her stitched-up, dutiful life. The next day the same papers were crowing about the way the proper princess had brought noted love cheat Rodolfo to heel, presumably with the sheer force of her *goodness*. It didn't matter what story the papers told; the people ate it up. They loved it.

Natalie, meanwhile, was miserable. And alone.

Everything was in ruins all around her—it was just too bad her body didn't know it.

Because it wanted him. So badly it kept her up at night. And made her hoard her vivid, searing memories of Rome and play them out again and again in her head. In her daydreams. And all night long, when she couldn't sleep and when she dreamed.

She was terribly afraid that it was all she would ever have of him.

The longer she didn't hear from Rodolfo or see him outside of the tabloids, the more Natalie was terrified that she'd destroyed Valentina's marriage.

Her future. Her destiny. That come the wedding day, there would be no groom at the altar. Only a princess bride and the wreck Natalie had made of her life.

Because she was a twin that shouldn't exist. A twin that couldn't exist, if Rodolfo had been right in Rome.

Do you suppose the king happily looked the other way while Queen Frederica swanned off with a stolen baby? he'd asked, and God help her, but she could still see the contempt on his face. It still ricocheted inside of her, scarring wherever it touched.

And it was still a very good question.

One afternoon she locked herself in Valentina's bedroom, pulled out her mobile and punched in her mother's number from memory.

Natalie and her mother weren't close. They never had been, and while Natalie had periodically wondered what it might be like to have the mother/daughter bond so many people seemed to enjoy, she'd secretly believed she was better off without it. Still, she and Erica were civil. Cordial, even. They might not get together for holidays or go off on trips together or talk on the phone every Sunday, but every now and then, when they were in the same city and they were both free, they had dinner. Natalie wasn't sure if that would make pushing Erica for answers harder or easier.

"Mother," she said matter-of-factly after the perfunctory greetings—all with an undercurrent of some surprise because they'd only just seen each other a few months back in Barcelona and Natalie wasn't calling from her usual telephone number—were done. "I have to ask you a very serious question."

"Must you always be so intense, Natalie?" her mother asked with a sigh that only made her sound chillier, despite the fact she'd said she was in the Caribbean. "It's certainly not your most attractive trait."

"I want the truth," Natalie forged on, not letting her mother's complaint distract her. Since it was hardly anything new. "Not some vague story about the evils of some or other Prince Charming." Her mother didn't say anything to that, which was unusual. So unusual that it made a little trickle of unease trail down Natalie's back...but what did she have to fear? She already knew the answer. She'd just been pretending, all this time, that she didn't. "Is your real name Frederica de Burgh, Mother? And were you by chance ever married to King Geoffrey of Murin?"

She was sitting on the chaise in the princess's spacious bedroom with the laptop open in front of her, looking at pictures of a wan, very unsmiling woman, pale with copper hair and green eyes, who had once been the Queen of Murin. Relatively few pictures existed of the notorious queen, but it really only took one. The woman Natalie knew as Erica Monette was always tanned. She had dark black hair in a pixie cut, brown eyes and was almost never without her chilly smile. But how hard could it be, for a woman who didn't want to be found or connected to her old self, to cut and dye her hair, get some sun and pop in color contacts?

"Why would you ask such a thing?" her mother asked.

Which was neither an answer nor an immediate refutation of her theory, Natalie noted. Though she thought her mother sounded a little...winded.

She cleared her throat. "I am sitting in the royal palace in Murin right now."

"Well," Erica said after a moment bled out into several. She cleared her throat, and Natalie thought that was more telling than anything else, given that her mother didn't usually do emotions. "I suppose there's no use in telling you not to go turning over rocks like that. It can only lead to more trouble than it's worth."

"Explain this to me," Natalie whispered, because it was that or shout, and she wasn't sure she wanted to give in to that urge. She wasn't sure she'd stop. "Explain *my life* to me. How could you possibly have taken off and gone on to live a regular life with one of the King's children?"

"I told him you died," her mother said matter-of-factly. So matter-of-factly, it cut Natalie in half. She couldn't even gasp. She could only hold the phone to her ear and sit there, no longer the same person she'd been before this phone call. Her mother took that as a cue to keep going, once again sounding as unruffled as she always did. "My favorite maid took you and hid you until I could leave Murin. I told your father one of the twins was stillborn and he believed it. Why wouldn't he? And of course, we'd hid the fact that I was expecting twins from the press, because Geoffrey's mother was still alive then and she thought it was unseemly. It made sense to hide that there'd been a loss, too. Geoffrey never liked to show a weakness. Even if it was mine."

A thousand questions tracked through Natalie's head then. And with each one, a different emotion, each one buffeting her like its own separate hurricane. But she couldn't indulge in a storm. Not now. Not when she had a charity event to attend in a few short hours and a speech to give about its importance. Not when she had to play the princess and try her best to keep what was left of Valentina's life from imploding.

Instead, she asked the only question she could.

"Why?"

Erica sighed. And it occurred to Natalie that it wasn't just that she wasn't close to her mother, but that she had no idea who her mother was. And likely never would. "I wanted something that was mine. And you were, for a time, I suppose. But then you grew up."

Natalie rubbed a trembling hand over her face.

"Didn't it occur to you that I would find out?" she managed to ask.

"I didn't see how," Erica said after a moment. "You were such a bookish, serious child. So intense and studious. It wasn't as if you paid any attention to distant European celebrities. And of course, it never occurred to me that there was any possibility you'd run into any member of the Murinese royal family."

"And yet I did," Natalie pushed out through the constriction in her throat. "In a bathroom in London. You can imagine my surprise. Or perhaps you can't."

"Oh, Natalie." And she thought for a moment that her mother would apologize. That she would try, however inadequately, to make up for what she'd done. But this was Erica. "Always so intense."

There wasn't much to say after that. Or there was, of course—but Natalie was too stunned and Erica was too, well, *Erica* to get into it.

After the call was over, Natalie sat curled up in that chaise and stared off into space for a long time. She tried to put all the pieces together, but what she kept coming back to was that her mother was never going to change. She was never going to be the person Natalie wanted her to be, whether Natalie was a princess or a secretary. None of that mattered, because it was Erica who had trouble figuring out how to be a mother.

And in the meantime, Natalie really, truly was a princess, after all. Valentina's twin with every right to be in this castle. It was finally confirmed.

And Rodolfo still isn't yours, a small voice inside her whispered. *He never will be, even if he stops hating you tomorrow. Even if he shows up for his wedding, it won't be to marry you.*

She let out a long, hard breath. And then she sat up.

It took a swipe of her finger to bring up the string of texts Valentina still hadn't answered.

It turns out we really are sisters, she typed. Maybe

you already suspected as much, but I was in denial.
So I asked our mother directly. I'll tell you that story
if and when I see you again.

She sent that and paused, lifting a hand to rub at
the faint, stubborn headache that wouldn't go away
no matter how much water she drank or how much
sleep she got, which never felt at all like enough.

I don't know when that will be, because you've fallen
off the face of the planet and believe me, I know
how hard it is to locate Achilles Casilieris when he
doesn't wish to be found. But if you don't show up
soon, I'm going to marry your husband and I didn't
sign up to pretend to be you for the rest of my life.
I agreed to six weeks and it's nearly been that.

She waited for long moments, willing the other
woman to text back. To give her some clue about…
anything. To remind her that she wasn't alone in
this madness despite how often and how deeply she
felt she was.

If you're not careful, you'll be Natalie Monette forever. Nobody wants that.

But there was nothing.
So Natalie did the only thing she could do. She got
to her feet, ignored her headache and that dragging
exhaustion that had been tugging at her for over a
week now, and went out to play Valentina.
Again.

CHAPTER ELEVEN

A FEW SHORT hours before the wedding, Rodolfo strode through the castle looking for his princess bride, because the things he wanted to say to her needed to be said in person.

He'd followed one servant and bribed another, and that was how he finally found his way to the princess's private rooms. He nodded briskly to the attendants who gaped at him when he entered, and then he strode deeper into her suite as if he knew where he was headed. He passed an empty media center and an office, a dining area and a cheerful salon, and then pushed his way through yet another door to find himself in her bedroom at last.

To find Valentina herself sitting on the end of the grand four-poster bed that dominated the space as if she'd been waiting for him.

She was not dressed in her wedding clothes. In fact, she was wearing the very antithesis of wedding clothes: a pair of very skinny jeans, ballet flats and a slouchy sort of T-shirt. There was an apricot-colored scarf wrapped around her neck several times, her hair was piled haphazardly on the top of her head and she'd anchored the great copper mess of it with a pair of oversize sunglasses. He stopped as the door shut behind him and could do nothing but stare at her.

This was the sort of outfit a woman wore to wander down to a café for a few hours. It was not, by any possible definition, an appropriate bridal ensemble for a woman who was due to make her way down the aisle of a cathedral to take part in a royal wedding.

"You appear to be somewhat underdressed for the wedding," he pointed out, aware he sounded more than a little gruff. Deadly, even. "Excuse me. I mean *our* wedding."

There was something deeply infuriating about the bland way she sat there and did nothing at all but stare back at him. As if she was deliberately slipping back into that old way she'd acted around him. As if he'd managed to push her too far away from him for her to ever come back and this was the only way she could think to show it.

But Rodolfo was finished feeling sorry for himself. He was finished living down to expectations, including his own. He was no ghost, in his life or anyone else's. After their conversation in Tissely, Ferdinand had appointed Rodolfo to his cabinet. He'd called it a wedding gift, but Rodolfo knew what it was: a new beginning. If he could manage it with his father after all these years and all the pain they'd doled out to each other, this had to be easier.

He'd convinced himself that it had to be.

"I am sorry, princess," he said, because that was where it needed to start, and it didn't seem to matter that he couldn't recall the last time he'd said those words. It was Valentina, so they flowed. Because he meant them with every part of himself. "You must know that above all else."

She straightened on the bed, though her gaze flicked away from his as she did. It seemed to take her a long time to look back at him.

"I beg your pardon?"

"I am sorry," he said again. There was too much in his head, then. Felipe. His father. Even his mother, who had refused to interrupt her solitude for a wedding, and no matter that it was the only wedding a child of hers would ever have. She'd been immovable. He took another step toward Valentina, then stopped, opening up his hands at his sides. "I spent so long angrily not being my brother that I think I forgot how to be me. Until you. You challenged me. You stood up to me. You made me want to be a better man."

He heard what he assumed were her wedding attendants in the next room, but Valentina only regarded him, her green eyes almost supernaturally calm. So calm he wondered if perhaps she'd taken something to settle her nerves. But he forgot that when she smiled, serene and easy, and settled back on the bed.

"Go on," she murmured, with a regal little nod.

"In my head, you were perfect," he told her, drift-

ing another step or so in her direction. "I thought
that if I could win you, I could fix my life. I could
make my father treat me with respect. I could clean
up my reputation. I could make myself the Prince I
always wanted to be, but couldn't, because I wasn't
my brother and never could be." He shook his head.
"And then at the first hint that you weren't exactly
who I wanted you to be, I lost it. If you weren't perfect, then how could you save me?"

That was what it was, he understood. It had taken
him too long to recognize it. Why else would he
have been so furious with her? So deeply, personally
wounded? He was an adult man who risked death for
amusement. Who was he to judge the games other
people played? Normally, he wouldn't. But then, he'd
spent his whole life pretending to be normal. Pretending he wasn't looking for someone to save him.
Fix him. Grant him peace.

No wonder he'd been destroyed by the idea that
the only person who'd ever seemed the least bit capable of doing that had been deliberately deceiving him.

"I don't need you to save me," he told her now. "I
believe you already have. I want you to marry me."

Again, the sounds of her staff while again, she
only watched him with no apparent reaction. He told
himself he'd earned her distrust. He made himself
keep going.

"I want to love you and enjoy you and taste you,
everywhere. I do not want a grim march through

our contractual responsibilities for the benefit of a fickle press. I want no *heir and spare,* I want to have babies. I want to find out what our life is like when neither one of us is pretending anything. We can do that, princess, can we not?"

She only gazed back at him, a faint smile flirting with the edge of her lips. Then she sat up, folding her hands very nicely, very neatly in her lap.

"I'm moved by all of this, of course," she said in a voice that made it sound as if she wasn't the least bit moved. It rubbed at him, making all the raw places inside him…ache. But he told himself to stand up straight and take it like a man. He'd earned it. Which wasn't to say he wouldn't fight for her, of course. No matter what she said. Even if she was who he had to fight. "But you think I'm a raving madwoman, do you not?"

And that was the crux of it. There was what he knew was possible, and there was Valentina. And if this was what Rodolfo had to do to have her, he was willing to do it. Because he didn't want their marriage to be like his parents'. The fake smiles and churning fury beneath it. The bitterness that had filled the spaces between them. The sharp silences and the barbed comments.

He didn't want any of that, so brittle and empty. He wanted to live.

After all this time being barely alive when he hadn't felt he deserved to be, when everyone thought he should have died in Felipe's place and he'd agreed, Rodolfo wanted to *live.*

"I do not know how to trust anyone," he told her now, holding her gaze with his, "but I want to trust you. I want to be the man you see when you look at me. If that means you want me to believe that there are two of you, I will accept that." His voice was quiet, but he meant every word. "I will try."

Still, she didn't say anything, and he had to fight back the temper that kicked in him.

"Am I too late, Valentina? Is this—" He cut himself off and studied her clothes again. He stood before her in a morning coat and she was in jeans. "Are you planning to run out on this wedding? Now? The guests have already started arriving. You will have to pass them on your way out. Is that what you planned?"

"I was planning to run out on the wedding, yes," she replied, and smiled as she said it, which made no sense. Surely she could not be so *flippant* about something that would throw both of their kingdoms into disarray—and rip his heart out in the process. Surely he'd only imagined she'd said such a thing. But Valentina nodded across the room. "But the good news is that *she* looks like she's planning to stay."

And on some level he knew before he turned. But it still stole his breath.

His princess was standing in the door to what must have been her dressing room, clad in a long white dress. There was a veil pinned to a shining tiara on her head that flowed to the ground behind her. She was so lovely it made his throat tight, and *her* green eyes were dark with emotion and shone with tears. He looked back to check, to make sure he wasn't losing his own mind, but the spitting image of her was still sitting on the end of the bed, still dressed in the wrong clothes.

He'd known something was off about her the moment he'd walked in. *His* princess lit him up. She gazed at him and he wanted to fly off into the blue Mediterranean sky outside the windows. More, he believed he could.

She was looking at him that way now, and his heart soared.

He thought he could lose himself in those eyes of hers. "How long have you been standing there?"

"Since you walked in the door," she whispered.

"Natalie," he said, his voice rough, because she'd heard everything. Because he really had been talking to the right princess after all. "You told me you were Natalie."

She smiled at him, a tearful, gorgeous smile that changed the world around. "I am," she whispered. "But I would have been Valentina for you, if that was what you wanted. I tried."

Valentina was talking, but Rodolfo was no longer listening. He moved to *his princess* and took her hands in his, and there it was. Fire and need. That sense of homecoming. *Life.*

He didn't hesitate. He went down on his knees before her.

"Marry me, Natalie," he said. Or begged, really.

Her hands trembled in his. "Marry me because you want to, not because our fathers decided a prince from Tissely should marry a princess from Murin almost thirty years ago. Marry me because, when you were not pretending to be Valentina and I was not being an ass, I suspect we were halfway to falling in love."

She pulled a hand from his and slid it down to stroke over his cheek, holding him. Blessing him. Making him whole.

"I suspect it's a lot more than halfway," she whispered. "When you said *mine,* you meant it." Natalie shook her head, and the cascading veil moved with her, making her look almost ethereal. But the hand at his jaw was all too real. "No one ever meant it, Rodolfo. My mother told me I grew up, you see. And everything else was a job I did, not anything real. Not anything true. Not you."

"I want to live," he told her with all the solemnity of the most sacred vow. "I want to live with you, Natalie."

"I love you," she whispered, and then she bent down or he surged up, and his mouth was on hers again. At last.

She tasted like love. Like freedom. Like falling end over end through an endless blue sky only with this woman, Rodolfo didn't care if there was a parachute. He didn't care if he touched ground. He wanted to carry on falling forever, just like this.

Only when there was the delicate sound of a throat

being cleared did he remember that Valentina was still in the room.

He pulled back from Natalie, taking great satisfaction in her flushed cheeks and that hectic gleam in her green eyes. Later, he thought, he would lay her out on a wide, soft bed and learn every single inch of her delectable body. He would let her do the same when he was sated. He estimated that would take only a few years.

Outside, the church bells began to ring.

"I believe that is our cue," he said, holding fast to her hand.

Natalie's breath deserted her in a rush, and Rodolfo braced himself.

"I want to marry you," she said fiercely. "You have no idea how much. I wanted it from the moment I met you, whether I could admit it to myself or not." She shook her head. "But I can't. Not like this."

"Like what?" He lifted her fingers to his mouth. "What can be terrible enough to prevent us from marrying? I haven't felt alive in two decades, princess. Now that I do, I do not want to waste a single moment of the time I have left. Especially if I get to share that time with you."

"Rodolfo, listen to me." She took his hand between hers, frowning up at him. "Your whole life was plotted out for you since the moment you were born. Even when your brother was alive. My mother might have made some questionable choices, but because she did, I got something you didn't. I lived exactly how I wanted to live. I found out what made me happy and I did it. That's what you should do. *Truly live.* I would hate myself if I stood between you and the life you deserve."

"You love me," he reminded her, and he slid his hand around to hold the nape of her neck, smiling when she shivered. "You want to marry me. How can it be that even in this, you are defiant and impossible?"

"Oh, she's more than that," Valentina chimed in from the bed, and then smiled when they both turned to stare at her. A little too widely, Rodolfo thought. "She's pregnant."

His head whipped back to Natalie and he saw the truth in his princess's eyes, wide and green. He let go of her, letting his gaze move over what little of her body he could see in that flowing, beautiful dress, even though he knew it was ridiculous. He could count—and he knew exactly when he'd been with her on that couch in Rome. To the minute.

He'd longed for her every minute since.

But mostly, he felt a deep, supremely male and wildly possessive triumph course through him like a brand-new kind of fire.

"Bad luck, *princesita*," he murmured, and he didn't try very hard to keep his feelings out of his voice. "That means you're stuck with me, after all."

"That's the point," she argued. "I don't want to be stuck. I don't want *you* to be stuck!"

He smiled at her, because if she'd thought she was

his before, she had no idea what was coming. He'd waited his whole life to love another this much, and now she was more than that. Now she was a family. "But I do."

And then, to make absolutely sure there would be no talking her way out of this or plotting something new and even more insane than the secret twin sister who was watching all of this from her spot on the bed, he wrenched open the door behind him and called for King Geoffrey himself.

"Make him hurry," he told the flabbergasted attendants as they raced to do his bidding. "Tell him I'm seeing double."

In the end, it all happened so fast.

King Geoffrey strode in, already frowning, only to stop dead when he saw Natalie and Valentina sitting next to each other on the chaise. Waiting for him.

Natalie braced herself as Valentina stood and launched into an explanation. She rose to her feet, too, shooting a nervous look over at Rodolfo where he lounged against one of the bed's four posters, because she expected the king to rage. To wave it all away the way Erica had. To say or do something horrible—

But instead, the King of Murin made a small, choked sound.

And then he was upon them, pulling both Natalie and Valentina into a long, hard, endless hug.

"I thought you were dead," he whispered into Natalie's neck. "She told me you were dead."

And for a long while, there was nothing but the church bells outside and the three of them, not letting go.

"I forget myself," Geoffrey said at last, wiping at his face as he stepped back from their little knot. Natalie made as if to move away, but Valentina gripped her hand and held her fast. "There is a wedding."

"My wedding," Rodolfo agreed from the end of the bed.

The king took his time looking at the man who would be his son-in-law one way or another. Natalie caught her breath.

"You were promised this marriage the moment you became the Crown Prince, of course, as your brother was before you."

"Yes." Rodolfo inclined his head. "I am to marry a princess of Murin. But it does not specify which one."

Valentina blinked. "It doesn't?"

The king smiled. "Indeed it does not."

"But everyone expects Valentina," Natalie heard herself say. Everyone turned to stare at her and she felt her cheeks heat up. "They do. It's printed in the programs."

"The programs," Rodolfo repeated as if he couldn't believe she'd said that out loud, and his dark gaze glittered as it met hers, promising a very specific kind of retribution.

She couldn't wait.

"It is of no matter," King Geoffrey said, sounding

every inch the monarch he was. He straightened his exquisite formal coat with a jerk. "This is the Sovereign Kingdom of Murin and last I checked, I am its king. If I wish to marry off a daughter only recently risen from the dead, then that is exactly what I shall do." He started for the door. "Come, Valentina. There is work to be done."

"What work?" Valentina frowned at his retreating back. But Natalie noticed she followed after him anyway. Instantly and obediently, like the proper princess she was.

"If I have two daughters, only one of them can marry into the royal house of Tissely," King Geoffrey said. "Which means you must take a different role altogether. Murin will need a queen of its own, you know."

Valentina shot Natalie a harried sort of smile over her shoulder and then followed the King out, letting the door fall shut behind her.

Leaving Natalie alone with Rodolfo at last.

It was as if all the emotions and revelations of the day spun around in the center of the room, exploding into the sudden quiet. Or maybe that was Natalie's head—especially when Rodolfo pushed himself off the bedpost and started for her, his dark gaze intent.

And extraordinarily lethal.

A wise woman would have run, Natalie was certain. But her knees were in collusion with her galloping pulse. She sank down on the chaise and watched instead, her heart pounding, as Rodolfo stalked toward her.

"Valentina arrived in the middle of the night," she told him as he came toward her, all that easy masculine grace on display in the morning coat he wore entirely too well, every inch of him a prince. And something far more dangerous than merely charming. "I never had a sister growing up, but I think I quite like the idea."

"If she appears in the dead of night in my bedchamber, princess, it will not end well." Rodolfo's hard mouth curved. "It will involve the royal guard."

He stopped when he was at the chaise and squatted down before her, running his hands up her thighs to find and gently cup her belly through the wedding gown she wore. He didn't say a word, he just held his palm there, the warmth of him penetrating the layers she wore and sinking deep into her skin. Heating her up the way he always did.

"Would you have told me?" he asked, and though he wasn't looking at her as he said it, she didn't confuse it for an idle question.

"Of course," she whispered.

"Yet you told me to go off and be free, like some dreadfully self-indulgent Kerouac novel."

"There was a secret, nine-month limit on your freedom," Natalie said, and her voice wavered a bit when he raised his head. "I was trying to be noble."

His gaze was dark and direct and filled with light.

"Marry me," he said.

She whispered his name like a prayer. "There are considerations."

"Name them."

Rodolfo inclined his head in that way she found almost too royal to be believed, and yet deeply alluring. It was easy to imagine him sitting on an actual throne somewhere, a crown on his head and a scepter in his hand. A little shiver raced down her spine at the image.

"I didn't mean to get pregnant," she told him, very seriously. "I'm not trying to trap you."

"The hormones must be affecting your brain." He shook his head, too much gold in his gaze. "You are already trapped. This is an arranged marriage."

"I wasn't even sick. Everyone knows the first sign of pregnancy is getting sick, but I didn't. I had headaches. I was tired. It was Valentina who suggested I might be pregnant. So I counted up the days and she got a test somewhere, and…"

She blew out a breath.

"And," he agreed. He smiled. "Does that truly require consideration? Because to me it sounds like something of a bonus, to marry the father of your child. But I am alarmingly traditional in some ways, it turns out."

Natalie scoffed at the famous daredevil prince who had so openly made a mockery of the very institutions he came from, saying such things. "What are you traditional about?"

His dark eyes gleamed. "You."

Her heart stuttered at that, but she pushed on. "And we've only had sex the one time. It could be a fluke. Do you want to base your whole life on a fluke?"

His gaze was intent on hers, with that hint of gold threaded through it, and his hands were warm even through layers and layers of fabric.

"Yes," he said. "I do."

It felt like a kiss, like fire and need, but Natalie kept going.

"You barely know me. And the little while you have known me, you thought I was someone else. Then when I told you I wasn't who you thought I was, you were sure I was either trying to con you, or crazy."

"All true." His mouth curved. "We can have a nice, long marriage and spend the rest of our days sorting it out."

"Why are you in such a rush to get married?" she demanded, sounding cross even to her own ears, and he laughed.

It was that rich, marvelous sound. Far better than Valentina's gold-plated chocolate. Far sweeter, far more complex and infinitely more satisfying.

Rodolfo stood then, rising with an unconscious display of that athletic grace of his that never failed to make her head spin.

"We are dressed for it, after all," he said. "It seems a pity to waste that dress."

She gazed up at him, caught by how beautiful he

was. How intense. And how focused on her. It was hard to think of a single reason she wouldn't love him wildly and fiercely until the day she died. Whether with him or not.

Better to be with him.

Better, for once in her life, to stay where she belonged. Where after all this time, she finally *belonged*.

"Natalie." And her name—her real name at last— was like a gift on his tongue. "The bells are ringing. The cathedral is full. Your father has given his blessing and your secret twin sister, against all odds, has returned and given us her approval, too, in her fashion. But more important than all of that, you are pregnant with my child. And I have no intention of letting either one of you out of my sight ever again."

She pulled in a breath, then let it out slowly, as if she'd already decided. As if she'd already stayed.

"I risked death," Rodolfo said then, something tender in his gaze. "For fun, princess. Imagine what I can do now I have decided to live."

"Anything at all," she replied, tears of joy in her voice. Her eyes. Maybe her heart, as well. "I think you're the only one who doesn't believe in you, Rodolfo."

"I may or may not," he said quietly. "That could change with the tides. But it only matters to me if you do."

And she didn't know what she might have done

then, because he held out his hand. The way he had on that dance floor in Rome.

Daring her. Challenging her.

She was the least spontaneous person in all the world, but Rodolfo made it all feel as if it was inevitable. As if she had been put on this earth for no other purpose but to love him and be loved by him in turn.

Starting right this minute, if she let it.

"Come." His voice was low. His gaze was clear. "Marry me. Be my love. All the rest will sort itself out, *princesita*, while we make love and babies with equal vigor, and rule my country well. It always does." And his smile then was brighter than the Mediterranean sun. "I love you, Natalie. Come with me. I promise you, whatever else happens, you will never regret it."

"I will hold you to that," she said, her heart in her voice.

And then she slipped her hand into Rodolfo's and let him lead her out into the glorious dance of the rest of their lives.

* * * * *

If you enjoyed
THE PRINCE'S NINE-MONTH SCANDAL
why not explore these other Caitlin Crews stories?

CASTELLI'S VIRGIN WIDOW
EXPECTING A ROYAL SCANDAL
THE RETURN OF THE DI SIONE WIFE
THE GUARDIAN'S VIRGIN WARD
BRIDE BY ROYAL DECREE
Available now!

And watch out for the second part of Caitlin's
SCANDALOUS ROYAL BRIDES duet,
coming June 2017!

#3537 THE PREGNANT KAVAKOS BRIDE
One Night With Consequences
by Sharon Kendrick
Ariston Kavakos makes impoverished Keeley Turner a proposition:
a month's employment on his island, at his command. Soon her
resistance to their sizzling chemistry weakens! But when there's a
consequence, Ariston makes one thing clear: Keeley *will* become
his bride...

#3538 A RING TO SECURE HIS CROWN
by Kim Lawrence
Why is Sabrina Summerville so drawn to her betrothed's dangerous
younger brother, Prince Sebastian? An abdication makes Sebastian
ruler—so he must marry Sabrina himself! If the sparks between
them are any indication, their marriage is going to be explosive...

#3539 SICILIAN'S BABY OF SHAME
Billionaires & One-Night Heirs
by Carol Marinelli
When chambermaid Sophie encounters Bastiano Conti, his raw
sexuality tempts her untouched body! Bastiano's conscience
flickers when he discovers that after their unforgettable
indiscretion, Sophie was left destitute and pregnant. He must
claim his child...by seducing Sophie into wearing his ring!

#3540 SALAZAR'S ONE-NIGHT HEIR
The Secret Billionaires
by Jennifer Hayward
Alejandro Salazar takes the opportunity to expose the Hargrove
family—by working in their stables! Alejandro mustn't be distracted
by Hargrove heiress Cecily's innocent passion. But when their
bliss results in pregnancy Alejandro will restore his family's honor...
with a diamond ring!

HPCNM0617RA

#3541 THE SECRET KEPT FROM THE GREEK
Secret Heirs of Billionaires
by Susan Stephens
Damon Gavros and Lizzie Montgomery's searing desire sweeps her back to their exquisite night eleven years ago! But Lizzie's hiding something, and Damon's determination to discover it is relentless. Until he finds out Lizzie's secret is his daughter!

#3542 THE BILLIONAIRE'S SECRET PRINCESS
Scandalous Royal Brides
by Caitlin Crews
Princess Valentina swaps places with her identical twin, but she quickly realizes that fooling her "boss" Achilles Casilieris is going to be difficult when he makes her burn with longing. Their powerful attraction will push Valentina's façade to the limit...

#3543 WEDDING NIGHT WITH HER ENEMY
Wedlocked!
by Melanie Milburne
Allegra Kallas both *detests* and longs for Draco Papandreou, so she's horrified when he's the only man who can save her family's business. Draco has a sinful plan: he'll make Allegra his wife and seduce her into his bed...

#3544 CLAIMING HIS CONVENIENT FIANCÉE
by Natalie Anderson
When Catriona breaks into her old family mansion to retrieve an heirloom, she doesn't expect to get caught by Alejandro Martinez! Kitty's recklessness ignites Alejandro's animal urges. So when Kitty is mistaken for his fiancée, he'll take full advantage—and unleash their hunger!

YOU CAN FIND MORE INFORMATION ON UPCOMING HARLEQUIN® TITLES, FREE EXCERPTS AND MORE AT WWW.HARLEQUIN.COM.

HPCNM0617RB

"You're offering to buy my baby? Are you out of your
mind?"

"I'm giving you the opportunity to make a fresh start."

"Without my baby?"

"A baby will tie you down. I can give this child everything
it needs," Ariston said, deliberately allowing his gaze to drift
around the dingy little room. "You cannot."

"Oh, but that's where you're wrong, Ariston," Keeley
said, her hands clenching. "You might have all the houses
and yachts and servants in the world, but you have a great
big hole where your heart should be—and therefore you're
incapable of giving this child the thing it needs more than
anything else!"

"Which is?"

"Love!"

Ariston felt his body stiffen. He loved his brother
and once he'd loved his mother, but he was aware of his
limitations. No, he didn't do the big showy emotion he

suspected she was talking about, and why should he, when he knew the brutal heartache it could cause? Yet something told him that trying to defend his own position was pointless. She would fight for this child, he realized. She would fight with all the strength she possessed, and that was going to complicate things. Did she imagine he was going to accept what she'd just told him and play no part in it? Politely dole out payments and have sporadic weekend meetings with his own flesh and blood? Or worse, no meetings at all? He met the green blaze of her eyes.

"So you won't give this baby up and neither will I," he said softly. "Which means that the only solution is for me to marry you."

He saw the shock and horror on her face.

"But I don't want to marry you! It wouldn't work, Ariston—on so many levels. You must realize that. Me, as the wife of an autocratic control freak who doesn't even like me? I don't think so."

"It wasn't a question," he said silkily. "It was a statement. It's not a case of if you will marry me, Keeley—just when."

"You're mad," she breathed.

He shook his head. "Just determined to get what is rightfully mine. So why not consider what I've said, and sleep on it and I'll return tomorrow at noon for your answer—when you've calmed down. But I'm warning you now, Keeley—that if you are willful enough to try to refuse me, or if you make some foolish attempt to run away and escape—" he paused and looked straight into her eyes "—I will find you and drag you through every court in the land to get what is rightfully mine."

Don't miss
THE PREGNANT KAVAKOS BRIDE
available July 2017 wherever
Harlequin Presents® books and ebooks are sold.

www.Harlequin.com

HARLEQUIN Presents.

Next month, look out for the final installment of the thrilling **The Secret Billionaires** trilogy! Three extraordinary men accept the challenge of leaving their billionaire lifestyles behind. But in *Salazar's One-Night Heir* by Jennifer Hayward, Alejandro must also seek revenge for a decades-old injustice…

Tycoon Alejandro Salazar will take any opportunity to expose the Hargrove family's crime against his—including accepting a challenge to pose as their stable groom! His goal in sight, Alejandro cannot allow himself to be distracted by the gorgeous Hargrove heiress…

Her family must pay, yet Alejandro can't resist innocent Cecily's fiery passion. And when their one night of bliss results in an unexpected pregnancy Alejandro will legitimize his heir and restore his family's honor…by binding Cecily to him with a diamond ring!

The Secret Billionaires

Challenged to go undercover—but tempted to blow it all!

Di Marcello's Secret Son
by Rachael Thomas

Xenakis's Convenient Bride
by Dani Collins
Available now!

Salazar's One-Night Heir
by Jennifer Hayward
Available July 2017!

Stay Connected:

www.Harlequin.com

f /HarlequinBooks

t @HarlequinBooks

p /HarlequinBooks

HP06080